THE PUFFIN BOOK OF
MAGICAL
INDIAN MYTHS

ANITA NAIR

ILLUSTRATED BY
ATANU ROY

PUFFIN BOOKS

PUFFIN BOOKS
Published by the Penguin Group
Penguin Books India Pvt. Ltd, 11 Community Centre, Panchsheel Park, New Delhi 110 017, India
Penguin Group (USA) Inc., 375 Hudson Street, New York, New York 10014, USA
Penguin Group (Canada), 90 Eglinton Avenue East, Suite 700, Toronto, Ontario, M4P 2Y3, Canada
(a division of Pearson Penguin Canada Inc.)
Penguin Books Ltd, 80 Strand, London WC2R 0RL, England
Penguin Ireland, 25 St Stephen's Green, Dublin 2, Ireland (a division of Penguin Books Ltd)
Penguin Group (Australia), 250 Camberwell Road, Camberwell, Victoria 3124, Australia (a division of
Pearson Australia Group Pty Ltd)
Penguin Group (NZ), 67 Apollo Drive, Rosedale, North Shore 0632, New Zealand (a division of Pearson
New Zealand Ltd)
Penguin Group (South Africa) (Pty) Ltd, 24 Sturdee Avenue, Rosebank, Johannesburg 2196, South Africa

Penguin Books Ltd, Registered Offices: 80 Strand, London WC2R 0RL, England

First published in Puffin by Penguin Books India 2007

10 9 8 7 6 5 4 3 2 1

ISBN-13: 978-0-14333-004-2   ISBN-10: 0-14333-004-7

Typeset in Bembo by Eleven Arts, New Delhi
Printed at Thomson Press (India) Ltd., India

For Maitreya,
star of my life
—A.N.

To Babu and Ma for all their support in my creative pursuits.
Amma, Papa and Varsha for opening up our mythologies for me.
My gang of friends: Suranjana, Rahul, Vedobroto, Anurima,
Anirudh and Antara (nephews and nieces), Siddharth
(grandnephew), Amrita, Siddhant, Prarthana and Prerna.
—A.R.

Contents

Acknowledgements

My mother, Soumini, and grandmother Janaki fed my appetite for myths and legends. K. Gopalakrishnan, Assistant Professor Kathakali, Kerala Kalamandalam, Cheruthurthy, Kerala, in his own inimical manner added and embellished these myths with fresh insights and helped fill the gaps. When I began work on this book, it was their stories and their art of storytelling that I sought to recreate.

However, to make sure that these are authentic versions, I have used as reference pointers *A Classical Dictionary of Hindu Mythology and Religion, Geography, History and Literature* by John Dowson and *A Dictionary of World Mythology* by Arthur Cotterell.

Anita Nair

How the Sun Became Less Fierce

One night Aruna, the goddess of dawn and the mother of Surya the sun god, woke up from her sleep sweating and agitated. A voice had whispered to her that if she didn't take care, her son would leave her and wander away to some distant horizon. If that happened, the universe would forever be plunged in darkness.

In the morning, Surya was feeling restless. He felt he must set out on a long journey. So he announced to his mother that he was going out for a ride through the sky. Aruna hid her fear. Instead she flashed him a broad smile and said, 'Surya, my son, what a lovely idea! I think I will come with you. Would you like me to be your charioteer?'

Surya was very fond of his mother. Besides, he knew she was very good with horses. So he agreed, even though he had been looking forward to riding on his own.

Surya's chariot was drawn by seven horses, each with gleaming coats like brownish-red silk and adorned with tassels of gold. He climbed into the chariot and Aruna hoisted herself into the charioteer's seat.

She flicked the whip and the horses began to trot. Soon they were galloping through the skies. As the wind rushed through his hair Surya felt a tremendous sense of exhilaration. 'Mother, I don't feel so restless any more,' he screamed, and Aruna smiled back, saying, 'I know! I know!'

As they rode along, Aruna spotted a beautiful young girl in a garden full of flowers. She was singing and frolicking with her maids. Suddenly Aruna had an idea. She steered the chariot close to the garden and, just as she had hoped, she saw Surya and the girl look at each other.

Surya was not very tall but he had a body that was muscular and like burnished copper. When he smiled, its radiance melted even the hardest of hearts. Now he smiled at the girl, and she, enchanted by him, blushed shyly.

'Who is that?' Surya asked aloud.

'Sanjana,' Aruna said. 'Her father is Vishwakarma, the architect of the gods.'

'What a beautiful girl,' Surya said. 'She will make someone a wonderful wife.'

Aruna stopped the chariot and asked him, 'Would you like to marry her?'

Thus Surya and Sanjana's marriage was arranged. When the ceremony was over, Surya led his bride to his palace, and that was when their troubles began. Until then they hadn't been together, and now when Surya went to sit next to Sanjana, the heat of his radiance scorched her skin. It singed her flesh and burnt her insides. Sanjana couldn't stand the heat and she fainted. When Sanjana was roused by her maids flicking water on her face, she began to weep, 'I cannot stay with him. His radiance will burn me to ashes . . .'

Her maids helped her escape and, in her place, she left Chhaya or shade. Then, taking on the form of a mare, Sanjana fled to a dark forest. There she wandered stricken with sorrow and guilt. She loved her husband but, if he came close to her, she knew she would die. When Surya discovered that his wife had left the palace, he went in search of her. Soon he found Sanjana and, unwilling to be separated from her, he changed

himself into a stallion and went towards her. Sanjana was overjoyed to meet her husband in a form that was both pleasing and splendid. 'We shall never be separated again,' they said to each other.

But both Aruna and Vishwakarma were worried. The universe was in darkness. How could there be life without Surya spreading his light? 'What can we do?' Aruna asked. 'Surya will not consent to take his original form if it displeases Sanjana and poor Sanjana will be burnt to ashes even if he does.'

Vishwakarma thought for a while and said, 'There is only one thing to be done. I will have to chisel away some of his brilliant rays so that Sanjana and he can live together as husband and wife.'

So Vishwakarma went to the forest in which Surya and Sanjana now lived and cut away one-eighth of Surya's rays. The fiery trimmings fell to the earth. Two of them became Vishnu's disc and Shiva's trident. And since Surya had lost some of his radiance, it was possible for Sanjana to be with him. So they took their real forms and went back to live in their palace.

How the Lingam Was Born

Once there was a great argument between Brahma and Vishnu. Brahma said, 'I am the creator of this universe.'

Vishnu disagreed. 'No, you are not. I am,' he said.

As the intensity of the argument grew, all the gods assembled to watch who would win and the whole world came to a standstill. The wind wouldn't blow and water wouldn't flow. The sun and the moon shone at the same time. The people on the earth were frightened and began to pray to the supreme power to rescue them from this earth that had become hell.

Despite the cries of the world, Vishnu and Brahma continued to debate when, suddenly, from the depths of the cosmic ocean rose a great black stone. Crowned with flames, the black stone rose higher and higher till it was even higher than Mount Sumeru, the tallest mountain in the world.

All the gods watched in awe as the stone continued to grow. Even Brahma and Vishnu forgot their argument. Unable to contain their curiosity, they decided to investigate. Brahma became a swan and soared upwards while Vishnu became a boar and dived downwards. They prowled hither and thither, seeking the power of the stone. Suddenly the gigantic black stone split and, in a cave-like sanctuary, they saw Shiva seated. At that moment they realized that it was Shiva who was really the creator. From then on, the black stone or the lingam has always been worshipped as a symbol of Shiva's power.

How Mankind Was Saved from Extinction
Vishnu's First Avatar—The Matsya

Once upon a time there lived a good and holy man called Manu. But Manu was not happy because everyone around him, including his wife and children, were dishonest and wicked people. They laughed at his honest ways and taunted him for being a silly fool. But Manu refused to be swayed by their words and went about life in a quiet and righteous fashion.

Sometimes though, he would become very sad and desperate and then he would fold his hands in prayer and beseech the gods he prayed to every day, 'When will you take me away from these evil people? Is there to be no end to my suffering?'

Every morning, just before he sat down to eat his breakfast, Manu would fetch a small pot of water from the well to wash his hands. One morning as he poured water over his hands, he heard a tiny voice cry, 'Help! Help!'

Surprised, Manu looked around him and into the well. But he could see no one. Then he looked into the pot of water and in it was a tiny horned fish. As Manu watched, the fish opened its mouth and spoke to him in human voice, 'Preserve me and I will preserve you!'

Manu smiled and said, 'Don't worry, I shall not harm you. But how will you help me? You are so tiny that a frog can swallow you in one gulp.'

The fish swam a full circle and said, 'I cannot reveal the future to you but preserve me and I shall preserve you . . .'

So Manu left the fish in the little pot and put it away in a safe place. He knew if his children saw the fish, they would kill it just for fun. Every day Manu fed the fish and it talked to him about life and the importance of being a good human being. The fish grew rapidly and soon he had to move it to a tank at the bottom of his garden. But the fish continued to grow and so he moved it to a nearby lake. But it wouldn't stop growing and Manu turned to the fish for help, 'You will soon be bigger than the lake . . . Where shall I keep you now?'

'Take me to the ocean and come to see me every day. Soon it will be time for me to fulfil the purpose for which I was sent here,' the fish said and Manu did as it asked him to.

The ocean was a few hours away from his house. After the fish moved to the ocean, Manu would go there every evening with a bag of puffed rice. When he scattered the rice on the waves, the fish would appear before him.

One evening, it was waiting for Manu and when he walked into the waves, the fish said, 'Manu, the time has come for you to plan your escape. I want you to build a ship and keep in it the seed of every living being. You too must live in it. Do not stay in your house once the ship is ready.'

Manu was bemused by the fish's orders. But he trusted the fish greatly. By now Manu had realized that it was no ordinary creature. So he went to the forest and set

about chopping some sturdy trees. As he planed the branches and built his ship, his family and neighbours mocked him.

'Ho, ho, ho, going somewhere, are you?' one man said.

'What a fool he is! He's building a ship so far away from the sea. How do you plan to get it into the water? Will you wait for the rains to sweep it away? Ha, ha, ha . . .' his family laughed.

But Manu went about his task. Soon the ship was built and he began to live in it.

'He's gone mad!' his wife shrieked. 'Why has he stopped living in his house and started living in a ship that's not even on the sea?'

But Manu refused to get angry and continued to live in the ship. Every evening he went to meet the fish, which had grown as big as a hill now. 'Tonight's the night,'

the fish said. 'There will be a great storm and the flood waters will destroy all living creatures. Stay in your ship and I shall come for you.'

Manu rushed home to warn his family and the whole town. 'Come into my ship. You will be safe there. The flood waters will kill all of you,' he cried. But no one would listen to him.

That night, a great storm blew. It was a storm so powerful that no one had seen anything like it before. Rain poured down in torrents, lightning flashed continuously, and the waters of the ocean rose higher and higher. Soon the whole world was submerged. No man, woman or child survived, except Manu, who stayed dry and warm in his ship that floated on the surface of the rising water.

The fish arrived when the storm was at its peak. 'Manu,' it said, 'fasten a cable from the ship to my horn.'

Manu did as the fish asked and it towed his ship through the waters. They sailed high above the Himalayan peaks and the tall mountains of the world. The journey took many days and years and Manu began to feel lonely. He missed human company. 'Is the world to end with me?' he worried. 'Am I to be the last man on earth? Please, gods, help me. I would like to have some children, to love and protect and to leave the legacy of life.'

So Manu was granted a wife, and when the flood receded, they went back to live on the earth. Their children became the ancestors of mankind. As for the fish—Matsya—it was none other than Vishnu, the preserver of the universe.

The Churning of the Cosmic Ocean
Vishnu's Second Avatar—The Kurma

In the deluge, some of the rarest things in the world were swept under the waters. Much of that which was precious and irreplaceable was washed away. The gods decided to try and retrieve them. But they knew it would be an impossible feat unless they had help. So a delegation of gods went to the asuras to ask for their assistance. The asuras agreed to help, for they too desired some of the rare treasures, especially amrita, the nectar of life, which would make them immortal.

It was time to begin the search. But how would they reach into the vast depths of the ocean where the precious things now lay? 'We should churn the ocean, for only then will the rare objects float to the surface,' Brahma said.

So the gods asked the great serpent Vasuki to let them use its strong coils as the rope. The mountain Mandara would be the churn. Varuna, the

lord of night and the oceans, was asked to hold the mountain steady so that the churning could begin.

But he found the mountain much too heavy for him and had to give up. He fell on the ground, sweat running down his brow and chest. 'I can't do this,' he gasped, too tired to even speak.

The gods now needed to find someone else to hold it.

Vishnu's anxiety for the churning to start was greater than anyone else's for he knew that his consort Lakshmi was hidden somewhere in the cosmic ocean. Since a base was required to fix the mountain to the ocean bed, Vishnu offered to help. He took the form of Kurma—a giant tortoise—and his back, the tortoise shell, became the pivot for the mountain.

The serpent Vasuki was twisted around the mountain. The gods took hold of the serpent's head, and the asuras grabbed the tail end. Together they set about churning the ocean. And with it both good and bad began to emerge from the deep waters.

The great tugging and pulling of the serpent against the mountain caused Vasuki to exhale heavily and his breath emerged as a thick mist. That was how the clouds were born. The clouds burst into rain and fell on the gods, who welcomed the cooling showers. However, when the snake started spouting poison, many died.

The movement of the mountain killed many animals in the sea. But the rubbing of the serpent against the mountain squeezed the juices from the medicinal plants growing on its slopes. These juices ran down the slopes into the sea, which revived the

sea creatures. The rubbing also set off many fires, and Indra, the lord of lightning, had to make the rains come again to put out the fires.

Then, as the gods and the asuras continued with the churning, from the waters emerged the wondrous things which had been lost. First emerged Kamadhenu, the cow of plenty. It was given to Vashishta, the officiating priest. Then came Airavata, the stately white elephant, and Uchchaih-sravas, a wonderful horse, which were both claimed by Indra. Then emerged Sura, the goddess of wine, and following her from the whirlpool sprang the Parijata tree, which Indra said would be kept in heaven so that all celestial beings might enjoy its delicate fragrance. Then came Rambha, and the other celestial nymphs who later became dancers in Indra's court; next came the moon, which Shiva seized and wore as a hair ornament.

The gods and the asuras churned the ocean for a thousand years and still there was no sight of the nectar which was what they were really seeking. Instead, what came up was visha or poison. The snake gods drank as much of the poison as they could, but there was still so much left that it looked as if it would strike them all dead with its fumes. To prevent this, Shiva drank up all the poison, which lodged in his throat, turning his neck blue in colour. Now with renewed vigour, the churning began again. Shankha, the conch of victory, emerged, as did Kaustubha, a priceless jewel. Finally from amidst the froth, Lakshmi rose, with a lotus in her hand. Along with her, the ocean yielded the much-prized water of life. Wearing white robes, the god of medicines, Dhanwantri, appeared, bearing the jar of amrita in his palm.

The churning finally came to an end and the asuras now discovered that almost everything had been claimed for their own by the gods. This angered them so much that they snatched the pot of amrita and a battle started.

Shiva decided to intervene and said, 'Since both the gods and the asuras have worked equally hard to churn the ocean, I suggest that the nectar too be divided equally.'

'But who will divide the amrita?' everyone asked.

At that moment a beautiful woman appeared. Nobody had seen such loveliness before and all were dazzled. She said her name was Mohini. She smiled at them and said, 'Allow me to divide the water of life.'

Both the gods and the asuras agreed.

'Since the gods are elder to the asuras, they must be served first,' she said. The asuras were so enchanted by her that they agreed to that as well.

Everyone sat down in two rows with their plates in front of them. Mohini started serving the gods first, and since there were thirty-three of them, all that was left after they had been served were a few drops, which she poured down her own throat.

Just then the moon and the sun, who knew Mohini was actually Vishnu, spotted that Rahu, an asura who had disguised himself as a god, was sitting with them and had been served a portion of the amrita. They told Vishnu, who promptly hurled his sudarshan chakra at Rahu and cut off his throat. But the nectar had already slid down his throat, so his head and body remained alive separately. The head was called Rahu and the body, Ketu. Since then Rahu wreaks revenge on the moon and the sun by occasionally swallowing them up and plunging the world into darkness. But he cannot hold them for long and they always reappear. We call this an eclipse.

When the asuras realized that Vishnu had tricked them to ensure that only the gods became immortal, they were furious. Another battle started. But the asuras were tired after the churning and the gods were stronger than ever after having consumed the amrita. And so the asuras were defeated once again.

How the Earth Was Dredged Back
Vishnu's Third Avatar—The Varaha

Hiranyaksha and Hiranyakashipu were asura twins. They were groomed to be the chiefs of the asuras when they grew up. Even as children, they hated the gods and promised themselves that they would defeat them when they grew up.

One day Hiranyaksha, the older twin, had an idea. 'It is the people on the earth who give these gods delusions of grandeur. If there was no earth, then who would remain to pray to these gods,' he thought.

No sooner than he realized this than Hiranyaksha set off to destroy the earth. He dragged the earth to the bottom of the ocean and stood there holding it close to his chest.

'What shall we do now?' said one of the gods as they all gathered together. 'All those millions of people, birds, animals, trees, flowers . . . everything is at the bottom of the ocean. How can we bring it all back?'

'Even if we go to the ocean bed, how can we take on Hiranyaksha? He is stronger than all of us put together,' said another god.

Vishnu decided to fight Hiranyaksha. He assumed the form of Varaha, a gigantic boar, and swam to the bottom of the ocean. He challenged Hiranyaksha, and the ensuing battle continued for a thousand years.

Finally Vishnu slew the asura. Picking up the earth with his horns, he tossed it back to the surface. As soon as the earth was restored to its place, the birds sang as they did at the crack of dawn, the animals shook themselves awake from their long sleep, the leaves began to rustle and even the spider that had paused for more than a thousand years began to weave its web. And the people went about their lives as they used to. All was well again.

The Killing of Hiranyakashipu
Vishnu's Fourth Avatar—Narasimha

When Hiranyakashipu discovered that his twin had been killed by Vishnu, he decided to obtain a boon that would make him indestructible so that a similar fate would not befall him. To achieve this, he began a long penance to appease Shiva.

When Shiva finally appeared before him and offered him a boon, Hiranyakashipu asked that he should be made invincible.

'Even though you have proved your devotion to me, that I cannot promise,' Shiva said.

'In that case, I would like you to give me a boon that will ensure I cannot be destroyed either by man or animal, neither indoors nor outdoors, neither at day nor night, neither by poison nor weapon,' Hiranyakashipu said.

Shiva looked at him carefully, then smiled and said, 'So be it!'

Hiranyakashipu was certain that no one could defeat him now. The king of the asuras began his wars against the gods. He went to battle with Indra and wrested heaven away from him. There he began to dwell and rule heaven, the earth and the netherworld as if he were its only lord.

The gods went pleading to Shiva, who was in deep meditation, to help them. Shiva opened his eyes and said, 'You will have to endure your suffering for some more time. Hiranyakashipu's end is drawing near.'

The king of the asuras had a son named Prahlada. Hiranyakashipu was very fond of his son but his fondness turned to irritation when he discovered that his son was an ardent devotee of Vishnu. 'Who is this Vishnu fellow?' he bellowed. 'There is only one lord in this universe and that is I, your father, Hiranyakashipu. If you wish to worship someone, then repeat after me, "Om namo Hiranyakashipu!"'

But Prahlada refused to say such a prayer and continued with his prayers to Vishnu.

Hiranyakashipu watched his son's devotion and grew angrier and angrier. 'He is not my son,' he thundered. 'He is a traitor. Like all traitors, he deserves to die.'

Hiranyakashipu ordered that a rogue elephant be brought and made to trample the boy. But when the elephant saw Prahlada and heard him mutter, 'Narayana, Narayana,' it fell to its knees and dropped a garland of wild flowers around the boy's neck.

Angered by this failure, Hiranyakashipu let loose poisonous snakes on the boy's bed when he was fast asleep. But the snakes merely stood guard around the boy. When Prahlada woke up, they went away without harming him.

But the king was not ready to give up. He lit a pyre and had Prahlada thrown into it. Prahlada stood with his eyes closed, his hands folded in prayer, and continued to say, 'Narayana! Narayana!' Suddenly, a huge thunderstorm arrived out of the clear skies and sheets of rain put out the flames.

Furious, Hiranyakashipu dragged his son to the palace. 'Who is this Narayana? Where does he live?' he asked the boy.

'Narayana lives everywhere,' the boy said.

'Does he live here?' the asura demanded, slamming a door. 'Or does he live here?' he said, pushing down a table. 'Or is he crouched inside this pillar?' he asked, smashing the pillar with his mace.

The pillar fell apart and from it emerged a strange-looking creature. It was Narasimha, half man and half lion. It had the head and claws of a lion and the body of a man.

When Prahlada saw the apparition, he recognized instantly that the half man–half lion was Vishnu. He fell on the ground and exclaimed joyously, 'Oh, my lord, you are finally here!'

As the assembled courtiers watched in amazement, Narasimha grabbed Hiranyakashipu and dragged him towards the door of the palace. He paused on the threshold. For there it was neither indoors nor outdoors. Then, with his claws, that were neither weapon nor poison, and at twilight, which was neither day nor night, he ripped open Hiranyakashipu's stomach and pulled his intestines out.

Thus did Vishnu kill the tyrant Hiranyakashipu, but without breaking any of Shiva's promises.

Prahlada became the king of the asuras, returned heaven to Indra and made his subjects happy till his death.

How King Bali Lost His Kingdom
Vishnu's Fifth Avatar—Vamana

King Bali was the grandson of Prahlada and was as noble and pious as his grandfather. He ruled the asuras well and tried to curb their violent behaviour.

Unlike his ancestors, King Bali sought supremacy over heaven and earth by non-violent means. Instead of going to battle with the gods, he undertook rigorous penance and by the strength of his dedication and virtue, he wrested heaven away from Indra. Soon he was king of the three worlds and everyone on the earth loved him dearly. There never had been such a noble king as Bali, they said.

The gods soon grew jealous of Bali and feared that they would lose their standing if Bali continued to reign. 'The people don't turn to us in times of trouble

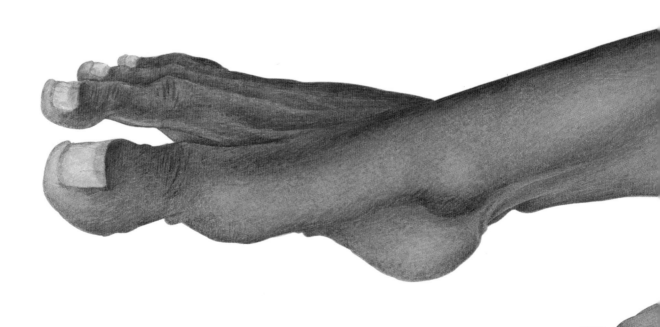

because Bali takes such good care of them. Soon they will forget that we exist. Moreover, he continues to accrue such blessings that he will remain lord of the three worlds forever,' they told Vishnu.

When Vishnu seemed unmoved by their fears, one of the gods added, 'Bali is a good king, but his children might not be such noble rulers. What then? They will destroy this universe if they inherit such power!'

So Vishnu decided to step in and save the gods from further humiliation. He was born to Sage Kashyapa and Aditi and was known as Vamana. Even as an adult, Vamana remained diminutive and it was as a little man he went to King Bali's court asking for alms.

King Bali received Vamana as though he were a very important guest and asked, 'What can I do for you? How can I be of service to you?'

Vamana looked up at the king and said, 'All I need is three feet of land!'

'Is that all?' Bali asked in surprise. 'Don't you need anything more?'

'Three feet of land will do,' Vamana said.

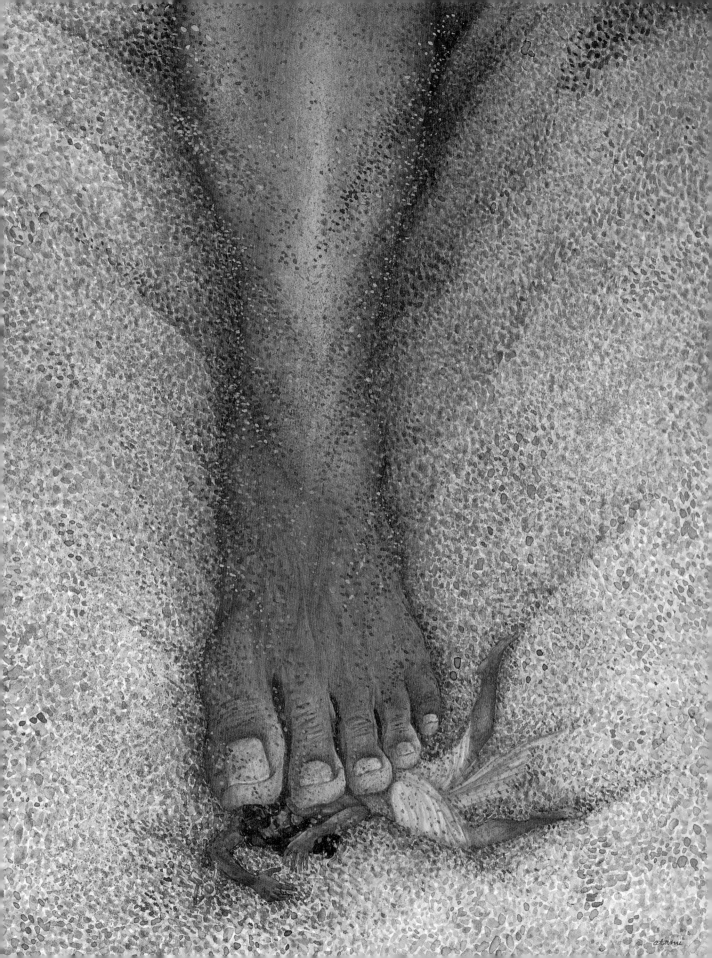

'Then it shall be yours. Do take it from wherever you want,' the king said, amused by the little man's modest request.

Then, as the king watched, Vamana began to grow rapidly. He multiplied in size until he was as tall as the trees, as tall as the mountains and finally as tall as the skies.

With his left foot, Vamana covered the earth. 'This is the first foot of land,' he said, his voice ringing through the skies. With his right foot, he covered heaven. 'This is the second foot. What is left, O king? Where shall I take my third foot of land from?'

King Bali realized that this was none other than Vishnu and that the third foot of land had to be found. So he fell on his knees and bent his head, 'All I have left is my head. Take this as the third foot of land,' he said with quiet dignity.

When the gods saw this, even they were moved to tears by Bali's humility and honour and rained flowers on Bali. But Vamana put his foot on the king's head and pressed him down into the netherworld. 'Henceforth, this shall be your kingdom,' he told King Bali.

As Bali was about to leave the earth for good, his grief-stricken subjects gathered to bid him farewell. When the king saw the tears in his people's eyes, he too was saddened. 'How can I stay away from my subjects?' he thought.

Bali turned to Vamana and said, 'I have one request before I leave. All I ask is that for one day in the year I be allowed to visit my people and know all is well with them.'

Vamana agreed.

Ever since, the king's subjects wait for his coming year after year. To this day, the people of Kerala welcome King Bali with a carpet of flowers every year. This day is known as Onam.

Why Sukanya Wed Chyavana

Chyavana was an old sage who lived in the forest by himself. One day, he began a penance that went on for several years. As he sat cross-legged, deep in meditation, termites built their nest around him. Soon the sage was completely covered, except for two holes that left his eyes visible.

Sukanya, the daughter of King Saryata, came to the forest with her friends. As they wandered picking flowers and fruit, they came to the spot where Chyavana sat concealed in a mound of mud.

Sukanya saw the small hillock and went close. 'What is this strange thing?' she asked her friends.

'That's an anthill,' said one of them.

'No, it's a termite's nest,' said another.

'But look at these two holes! Something glitters within,' Sukanya said.

'That's true. This is no ordinary anthill,' said the first girl.

'It must be the home of some rare creature; a gem-studded snake, perhaps,' said a third.

Sukanya stared at the glittering gems. Her desire to know what they were grew in intensity. Finally, she took a twig and poked the glittering objects.

Suddenly there was a scream of anguish and the anthill fell apart and from it emerged Chyavana with his eyes bleeding. The princess was frightened. What have I done, she thought, and fell at his feet. 'Forgive me, Your Holiness. I didn't know that you were there,' she cried.

But Chyavana refused to accept her apologies. 'You deserve to be punished for disturbing my penance and for hurting my eyes,' he growled.

'I meant no harm,' Sukanya pleaded. 'I saw the radiance of your eyes and thought they were rare jewels.'

But the sage refused to be placated.

Meanwhile King Saryata arrived on the spot and at one glance he understood that if he didn't step in and save the situation, he and his kingdom would be cursed.

So he too fell at the sage's feet. 'Please forgive my daughter,' he cried. 'And to make up for having hurt your eyes, I beg that you allow her to serve you for the rest of her life. Please take her as your wife and let her live here taking care of your every need.'

The princess's heart sank. What, marry this old and ugly man, she thought. But she said nothing, for she realized that if the sage didn't forgive them, a great calamity might occur and the kingdom would be doomed forever. So she swallowed her misery and smiled.

'You might offer her in marriage to me, but does she want me as her husband?' the sage demanded.

The king looked at his daughter.

She raised her eyes and said, 'If Your Holiness would have me, I will be privileged to be your wife.'

Chyavana looked at the young, beautiful princess and his heart softened. 'So be it,' he said.

And so Sukanya became the old and ugly Chyavana's wife and lived with him in the hermitage.

How Sukanya Thwarted the Ashwin Twins

The Ashwin twins were the sons of the sun god. They were young and handsome and looked so like each other that it was impossible to tell them apart. They were also the physicians of heaven.

One day in the course of their travels, they arrived at Chyavana's hermitage. The sage received them and said, 'I shall ask my wife Sukanya to take care of your needs.'

The twins were appalled to see that the sage's wife was the young and beautiful Sukanya. 'Why did you marry this old and ugly man?' they asked.

So she narrated the sequence of events.

'How do you bear it?' they asked her.

But Sukanya refused to speak anything against her husband or his looks. 'He makes me happy,' she said quietly.

One of the Ashwin twins said, 'Abandon him and one of us will be your husband. You do not deserve to be tied to a man as ugly as him. We are more suited to be your husband.'

But Sukanya refused. 'He is my husband and I shall remain with him. Besides, you are young and handsome now, how can you compare yourself to him? He must have been handsome in his youth too.'

The Ashwin twins smiled. 'That is true. Do you know who we are?' they asked.

She shook her head.

'We are the physicians of heaven,' they said laughing. 'So this is what we propose: we shall turn your husband into a young and handsome man, identical to us, and then you must choose from one of us.'

Sukanya thought about it and agreed.

The Ashwin twins asked Chyavana to go with them to a lake to bathe. When they returned after their bath, instead of two young men and one old man, three young men, all handsome and radiant, stood in front of her.

Sukanya smiled in delight, tinged with confusion.

'Now you must choose from one among us,' all three said together.

Sukanya closed her eyes and prayed for help. As she stood before the three young men who looked alike, she felt a strange power draw her towards one. She immediately understood he must be Chyavana. So she chose him.

The Ashwin twins accepted the decision. As for Chyavana, he was happy to be young and handsome. He told the twins, 'In time, I shall repay this favour.'

Meanwhile, in heaven, Indra was conducting a ceremony where all the gods would partake of soma, the divine drink. However, he refused to let the Ashwin twins drink the soma. 'The Ashwin twins are unreliable,' he said grimly. 'They don't behave like gods ought to. They wander among human beings and keep changing their forms as and when they please. I cannot allow it.'

The twins appealed to Chyavana for help. 'He will listen to you,' they said. So the sage went to meet Indra. But Indra refused to change his mind.

Chyavana could be as obstinate as Indra. He wanted to repay his debt to the twins and so he decided to perform a sacrifice that would procure the soma for them.

The other gods watched meekly but Indra was furious and rushed with a mountain in one hand and his thunderbolt in the other to crush Chyavana and disrupt the sacrifice.

As Indra approached, the sage sprinkled some water and stopped Indra's hands in mid-air. Then he created a fierce open-mouthed monster called Mada.

Mada had enormous teeth. His incisors and grinders were like jagged mountains. When he opened his jaws, one jaw enclosed the earth and the other, heaven.

With one terrible slow sound, Mada began to swallow the two worlds. There were screams and howls and cries of pain and fear as people began to slide down his gullet.

Indra and the gods were stuck at the root of Mada's tongue. Just as Mada was about to close his mouth, Indra cried, 'Your Holiness, listen to me. I am sorry for what I did.'

'Really?' asked the sage grimly.

Knowing there was no escape, Indra agreed to let the Ashwin twins drink the soma.

Thus Chyavana repaid the twins for their favour.

How Dadhyanch Saved the Earth

Atharvan was the eldest son of Brahma and it was to him Brahma first revealed Brahma-vidya or knowledge of the gods. Dadhyanch was the son of Atharvan. He was a sage whose breadth of knowledge was immense but it still didn't measure up to the scope of his father's. So Dadhyanch set about filling the gaps. After he performed many a severe penance, Indra appeared before him.

'What boon do you require?' Indra asked.

'Teach me the sciences you know,' the sage said.

Indra agreed to teach him certain sciences of healing. However, there was one condition. 'If you share this knowledge with anyone else, I shall cut off your head,' Indra told Dadhyanch. Dadhyanch agreed, and in return was taught all the celestial healing sciences.

Soon the Ashwin twins heard about the boon Dadhyanch had received. They went to him and begged and pleaded that he teach them the sciences too.

'How can I?' the sage said. 'Indra will cut my head off if he knows that I have disobeyed him.'

'We will take care of that,' the twins promised. 'Don't you trust us?'

So Dadhyanch taught them all that Indra had taught him. To save him from Indra's wrath, the twins replaced his head with a horse's. And waited.

When Indra heard that Dadhyanch had broken his promise, he struck off the sage's head. The twins immediately restored Dadhyanch's real head. And all was well.

As long as Dadhyanch lived on the earth, his presence was enough to control the asuras, but once he went to heaven, the asuras began to rule the earth, causing much chaos and distress.

Indra went to battle with them but was unable to defeat them.

'If only Dadhyanch had left something of his behind, I could have fashioned a weapon out of it to defeat the asuras,' he told the other gods.

Then the Ashwin twins reminded him of the horse's head, which had been Dadhyanch's for a while. 'It lies at the bottom of a lake near Kurukshetra,' they said.

Indra dredged the horse's head out. With the bones, he made weapons and foiled nine times ninety stratagems of the asuras. And peace was restored on earth.

Why Gadhinandana Became a Sage

King Gadhi had a daughter named Satyavati whom he gave in marriage to an old brahmin called Richika.

Since his wife was from the warrior race, Richika wanted her to have a child who would be more interested in religion and a religious life. So he gave her a plate of food which would ensure that the child would be born with those qualities.

As it happened, Satyavati's mother was also pregnant at the same time and he gave her a plate of food which would help her have a child with warrior-like qualities befitting a king's child.

However, the mother insisted that she and her daughter exchange the plates. As a result of this exchange, the king's son Gadhinandana, a kshatriya, was born with a great interest in religion and religious matters, and Satyavati bore Jamad-Agni, the father of Parasurama, the warrior-brahmin.

Gadhinandana grew up to be a mighty king. No one could defeat him in battle, and his kingdom was wealthy and powerful. Every now and then he went touring through his various kingdoms and, on one such visit, he came to a hermitage that was serene and beautiful. 'Who lives here?' he asked his minister and was told that it was the sage Vashishta's hermitage.

Meanwhile Sage Vashishta heard that there was a guest and went to greet him. The king and the sage talked for a great length of time and as it was drawing close to lunchtime, the king rose and told the sage, 'I must leave now. But it has been a great pleasure to have spent this morning with you.'

Vashishta gestured for the king to sit and said, 'Why leave in such a hurry? You must dine with us . . .'

The king smiled apologetically. 'If it was just me and a few ministers, I would have stayed gladly. But I have my army with me and it has to be fed as well.'

'Is that all?' the sage smiled. 'There is food enough for everyone here.'

Gadhinandana was surprised by the sage's words. How could a small ashram feed an entire army at such short notice? However, he did not want to offend Sage Vashishta, so he sent word to the army commanders to bring the men in.

As the king watched, the inmates of the hermitage produced a wondrous feast. Hundreds of dishes were served in gold bowls and silver plates. There were silk-covered chairs and cushions to sit on. The food was like nothing they had ever tasted before and there was as much as all of them could eat. When each one of them was replete, the king couldn't contain his curiosity.

'I have never eaten such a fine meal or seen anyone arrange a feast at such short notice. How did you manage to do it?' he asked the sage.

Vashishta smiled and waved his hand as though to dismiss the query. 'Aren't you satisfied? Why know where it came from?'

'The satisfaction would be complete if I knew the answer,' Gadhinandana replied.

Vashishta thought for a moment. Then he said, 'I have never told anyone outside the ashram about this, but I shall reveal my secret to you.'

He led the king to a lovely meadow where there was a cow with the head of a beautiful woman. 'This is Kamadhenu,' he said. 'She is one of the rarest treasures that emerged when the cosmic ocean was churned. As I was the officiating priest, she was given to me. She has the power to give people whatever they desire.'

The king looked at Kamadhenu and thought that she ought to belong to him. 'This wonder-cow deserves to live in a palace,' he said.

'Oh, I am very happy here,' Kamadhenu replied, sensing trouble.

'I don't mean that,' the king said. 'A wonder-cow like you will be a great asset in my palace.' He turned to the sage and said, 'Imagine the number of people who come visiting—kings, generals, sages, priests—a cow like this will ensure that they are provided the best. I must have her and I will give you whatever you want in return. Just name the price. A million cows or a thousand elephants? Gold and silver? Whatever . . .'

But the sage shook his head and said, 'I cannot let her go. She is like my own sister. I love her too dearly, and besides, we need her here. Every day we perform sacrifices and she provides us with the holy ingredients. If those sacrifices don't take place, the world will be plagued by many troubles.'

But the king was adamant and refused to see reason. He called ten of his men and said, 'Take this cow to my palace. Be careful how you handle her. No harm is to come to her.'

Kamadhenu watched sorrowfully as the soldiers hastened to take her away. 'Are you going to let me go?' she asked Vashishta.

'No, my dear sister. It is time for you to protect yourself, but see that you do not create more damage than necessary,' Vashishta said.

So the cow shook herself and from her hair dropped ten fully armed soldiers. They quickly attacked and defeated the king's men. Gadhinandana was both enraged and amazed. His desire to possess Kamadhenu grew more intense. He called for more men. Kamadhenu shook herself again and more men emerged, enough to match the number of soldiers the king had summoned.

When Kamadhenu withdrew from the battle, there was just one soldier left of the king's vast army.

Gadhinandana stood with his head bowed and said, 'These soldiers were the finest in the world. But even they were no match for the ones Kamadhenu brought forth. What power is it that makes her so strong?'

Vashishta shook his head. Gadhinandana was truly an unusual man. Here he was, a ruined man—for what is a king without his army?—and he was still seeking answers.

'I appreciate your spirit of inquiry. So it is my duty to give you an answer. This strength or power as you call it comes from within. In each one of us is a great vein of strength, an almost god-like power. All we need to do is seek and nothing will be impossible after that.'

The king looked at the sage as if he couldn't believe his ears. 'But how does one reach that inner power?'

'By concentrating and seeking that inner strength to the exclusion of everything else,' the sage said. Gadhinandana said, 'I understand. One day I too shall possess the power that you have and only then will I rest.'

The king advised his ministers to go back to his kingdom and rule it in his place. He gave away his royal clothing and donned the robes of a sage. He now had a single aim: he would not rest till he was Vashishta's equal.

How the King Became Vishwamitra

King Gadhinandana went deep into a forest on the slopes of a mountain and there, by the side of a stream, he performed rigorous austerities. He meditated for a thousand years and achieved such a perfect state of concentration that Shiva appeared before him and wanted to know why he was subjecting himself to such pains.

'I want to be Vashishta's equal. I want to have an army that matches his. I would like to possess and be able to use the Brahma-astra,' Gadhinandana said.

Shiva granted him these wishes.

The king summoned the army of fearless warriors bequeathed to him by Shiva and rushed to Vashishta's hermitage. 'I shall show the sage who is stronger,' he said to himself.

As the vast army drew closer, the inmates of the ashram began to fear what was to happen to them. 'Do not worry,' Vashishta said. 'Go about your duties. No harm shall come to any of you.'

When the king's archers began to shoot arrows at the hermitage, the arrows fell to the ground, bent and twisted. It was as if the hermitage was cloaked in a metal armour. The king and his men tried their best but to no avail.

Finally, Gadhinandana brought out the Brahma-astra, the deadliest of weapons which would find its target and raze it to ashes. But when he hurled it at the ashram, it had no effect.

Defeated, the king stood at the door of the hermitage and cried, 'Sage, tell me what makes you more powerful than me.'

Vashishta laughed. 'You are a warrior and will always remain one. So you seek blessings to destroy me. But I will not blame you for that. You are destined to behave that way.'

'I do not agree,' the king retorted. 'Our birth cannot decide how we behave. I shall prove to you that I too can be a brahma rishi just like you.'

The king retired to the forest and began another thousand years of penance. Brahma appeared before the king and said, 'You have proved yourself. Henceforth, you shall be called Vishwamitra.'

The king looked pleased but he was still not satisfied. 'What kind of rishi am I?' he asked.

'You shall be a raja rishi, a kingly sage,' Brahma said.

'But I want to be a brahma rishi. I want to be Vashishta's equal,' the king cried.

'You will be a raja rishi,' Brahma said and disappeared.

The king who was now known as Vishwamitra couldn't get Vashishta out of his mind. He began to look for ways to prove that he was Vashishta's equal or even superior.

Why the River Saraswati Disappeared

Once Sage Vishwamitra ordered River Saraswati to bring Vashishta to him.

The river pleaded with the sage. 'Please do not use me to settle your disputes. You are both great souls, how can I favour one more than the other?'

Vishwamitra grew angry and said, 'If you do not bring the sage to me, I shall curse that you remain dry forever.'

River Saraswati went to Vashishta and explained what had happened. Then she said, 'I do not care if he curses me. But I shall not take you to him. Instead I shall take you farther away from him.'

When Vishwamitra realized what had happened, he cursed the river that henceforth her waters would turn into blood. To escape the sage's wrath, Saraswati went underground and, to this day, has never come to the surface again.

Once there was a great drought. Crops failed, plants and trees withered, and there was no food anywhere. The brahmins, who were vegetarians, suffered more than other people who ate meat, as there was no food available anywhere for them. The need to find food kept them occupied, and in this relentless search they had no time to study the Vedas. Soon, the holy texts were forgotten.

The river Saraswati had a son called Saraswata, who was a brahmin. When this drought started, River Saraswati met her son secretly and said, 'Every day I shall feed you the fish that live in my subterranean waters. They shall keep you alive till such time as the drought passes.'

And so Saraswata lived on fish. He was the only brahmin who managed to keep up with his studies.

When the drought was over, the brahmins realized that they had forgotten the Vedas. 'What shall we do?' they asked each other.

Then someone said, 'Saraswata hasn't forgotten any of the Vedas. We should ask him to teach us.'

'How can we?' an old brahmin said. 'He has sinned. He has survived by eating fish. By going to him, we would be sinning too.'

Then another old brahmin said, 'We ought not to cut our nose to spite our face. Saraswata alone knows the Vedas. And a man who knows the Vedas is not a sinner. He did what he had to, to stay alive without committing a crime. He didn't steal or murder, he didn't take food from others and he didn't beg either. And that is a human being's prime duty—to try and stay alive without straying from the path of righteousness. I suggest that we ask Saraswata to help us.'

One section of them saw wisdom in the old man's words and went to Saraswata. And he in turn taught sixty thousand of them everything about the Vedas. To this day, the descendants of those sixty thousand men are known as Saraswat Brahmins.

Why a New Heaven Was Created for Trishankhu

Satya Vrata was a king of the sun dynasty. He was a good and pious man, and he looked after the interests of his subjects as though they were his children. All the people in his kingdom loved him dearly. They would often bless him and say, 'When he dies, his soul will surely go to heaven.'

King Satya Vrata heard their blessings and soon he became obsessed with a thought: 'Why is it that I should go to heaven only after I die? I would like to experience heaven the way I am. I would like to ascend to heaven with this body of mine.'

The more the king thought about it, the more convinced he was of the idea. So he decided to conduct a great sacrifice that would allow him to ascend to heaven with his body.

Finally, he broached the idea to his head priest, the sage Vashishta.

Vashishta laughed when he heard the king's desire. 'What is wrong with you? Don't you know that mortals cannot go to heaven in their bodies? Only the soul is permitted entry into heaven. Don't ask me to perform the impossible.'

King Satya Vrata was upset but he hid his anger at Vashishta's words and decided to visit Vashishta's sons. He hoped that they would be awed by him and agree to perform the sacrifice.

'Please make preparations for a great sacrifice. I want to ascend to heaven in my body,' he said, quite certain that they would do as he asked.

But Vashishta's sons became angry when they heard his request. 'How dare you come to us when our father has already said it is impossible? Don't you have any

sense of propriety? And for that you deserve to be cursed. Henceforth, the graveyard will be your home and tending to funeral pyres your duty. You are now a chandala.' Vashishta's sons cursed him and sent him on his way.

But the king, despite the humiliation and the curse, still wouldn't give up his dream. On his way back to the palace, he met the sage Vishwamitra.

'Why do you look so glum?' Vishwamitra asked the king.

When Satya Vrata explained his dilemma, Vishwamitra was secretly delighted. He still wanted to show Vashishta that he was his superior, and this seemed the perfect opportunity. He said, 'Is that all? Don't worry. I shall send you to heaven in your body.'

Satya Vrata was overjoyed.

Vishwamitra arranged for a great sacrifice and Satya Vrata sat at his side as they lit the holy fire and began chanting the various mantras. Soon the moment arrived when Satya Vrata began to ascend to heaven. Everyone watched in wonder as he rose through the air. They hailed Vishwamitra as the greatest sage ever.

Suddenly, however, all rejoicing stopped, for they could see a strange sight.

There was Satya Vrata coming back to earth head first. Vishwamitra raised his hand and stopped the king mid-flight. 'You fool, why are you coming back? What happened?' he demanded.

'When I reached heaven, Indra and the other gods wouldn't let me in. They said I couldn't come in there with my body and kicked me down!' said Satya Vrata sadly.

'How dare they?' Vishwamitra roared and sent the king back.

There ensued a contest of wills. The sage sent the king up and the gods kicked him back over and over again. The poor king was stuck in between and, to make matters worse, he didn't know if he was coming or going because he was still head down and feet up. Caught between heaven and earth, the king came to be known as Trishankhu, or he who is in limbo.

'I don't want to go to heaven. Please let me come back to the earth,' Trishankhu pleaded but Vishwamitra had set his heart on this and wouldn't let the king descend.

'In that case, let me at least stand on my feet,' poor Trishankhu pleaded, but Vishwamitra wasn't listening and so Trishankhu continued to be tossed like a ball between heaven and the earth.

Finally the sage and the gods arrived at a compromise and Vishwamitra created a whole new heaven for Trishankhu where he lived as an immortal being in his own body amidst stars and other celestial beings.

How Vishwamitra Rescued Sunashepas

King Ambarish of Ayodhya was about to conduct a great sacrifice. Indra, who was scared that the sacrifice would make the king even more powerful than he was, decided to prevent the sacrifice. So he carried the sacrificial animal away.

'What do we do now?' King Ambarish asked his officiating priests sadly.

They shook their heads and said in a grim voice, 'It saddens us to say this but the gods demand a greater price. Which means you have to make a human sacrifice, of a youth who is neither boy nor man, and someone who agrees to it without being forced into the decision. Nothing else will make up for what has happened!'

'Where shall I find a youth willing to sacrifice himself?' the king asked no one in particular. 'We do not know,' the priests said. 'You will have to find him yourself.'

So the king set out on his search and finally found a brahmin named Richika who had three sons. The king approached Richika and said, 'You have three sons. Give me one. This is for a worthy cause. In return, I shall pay you any price you want.'

Richika put his arm around his eldest son and said, 'I can't let my eldest son go. He is my favourite and he will continue my line.'

The mother clung to her youngest son and cried, 'I can't let him go either. He is my baby and I would die if anything happened to him.'

The middle son, Sunashepas, heard what his parents had to say and came forward with a sad face. 'O king,' he said, 'since neither of my parents seems to want me, I offer myself to you. Give them enough riches to live well and I shall be your human sacrifice.'

So the family was given a hundred thousand cows, ten million gold pieces and heaps of jewels and the king went away with Sunashepas.

On the way to the palace, they met Vishwamitra. The sage was Sunashepas's uncle and, when he saw the sorrow on the boy's face, he asked him what the matter was. Sunashepas explained.

Vishwamitra listened to the boy's tale in horror. 'Let him go,' he told the king. 'No human should be sacrificed and it is unfair to put this kind of pressure on the boy or his family. Can't this sacrifice be performed without murdering Sunashepas? Yes, that is what this is—murder. Cold-blooded murder!'

But the king refused to heed Vishwamitra's words. So Vishwamitra offered the king one of his sons. But the sons stared at their father angrily and said, 'How dare you propose to give one of us up in place of your nephew? We refuse to be sacrificed.' When Vishwamitra saw that his sons had no intention of going with the king, he lost his temper and cursed them, 'For disobeying your father, I curse you to become nomads with no home to call your own.'

Then he turned to his nephew and taught him two divine mantras. 'Repeat these during the time of the sacrifice and no harm will come to you,' he said.

At Ambarish's palace, Sunashepas was tied to the stake to be immolated. As the priests began the process of the sacrifice, Sunashepas closed his eyes and began to recite the two mantras which propitiated Vishnu and Indra. He said them with such sincerity that both the gods were pleased and granted him a long life. So Sunashepas escaped death and was henceforth known as Devarata.

How Vishwamitra Became a Brahma Rishi

Despite the various distractions, Vishwamitra hadn't given up his resolution to become a brahma rishi and continued to work towards that.

The gods decided to break his concentration. They sent a beautiful apsara called Menaka to distract him. Menaka was a dancer in Indra's court. She was so beautiful that no man could resist her.

Vishwamitra too was smitten by her beauty and grace. He stopped his penance to be with her. However, after a while he realized that this was why the gods had sent her. He promptly sent her away and resumed his penance.

The gods then sent an even more beautiful apsara, Rambha, and Vishwamitra was so enraged that he cursed her to be a stone figure for ten thousand years.

A little later when Vishwamitra saw the stone statue, he felt sad for what he had done. He realized he had acquired great powers to only use them up for seemingly useless reasons. He thought of his past: his squabbles with Vashishta, fighting the gods to let Trishankhu into heaven, cursing his sons and other such mishaps spurred by rage and pride. He decided that henceforth he would not let anger cloud his vision. He would seek to find peace. He began his austerities again with a new resolve.

Vishwamitra retired to a secluded forest and began meditating. He didn't speak, he didn't eat, he didn't even drink a drop of water and, at one point, breathed

only a tiny wisp of air. For a thousand years, he meditated and the gods began to fear that his concentration would reduce the world to ashes. They asked Brahma to intervene.

Finally it was time for Vishwamitra to break his fast. He gathered some fruits and sat down to eat. Just as he was about to begin, a beggar arrived. 'I'm hungry,' he cried. 'Please give me some food!'

Vishwamitra offered him all the food he had and said, 'This is all I have. But it is yours. I only wish I could have given you more and something better.'

For the first time Vishwamitra had forgotten who he was and all his lofty ambitions. He had behaved like a true sage.

The beggar, who was really Brahma in disguise, now revealed his true form to the sage. With a benevolent smile, he said, 'Through your hardship you have achieved what you sought. You deserve to be a brahma rishi, and henceforth you shall be known as one.'

Vishwamitra had finally achieved what he sought for so many years. But now he no longer had any desire to show his superiority to Vashishta. The two of them reconciled and became friends.

Later, Vishwamitra was to become one of the sapta rishis, a constellation that even to this day shines bright in the night sky.

How All Living Creatures Began to Blink

King Nimi of Mithila was preparing to have a grand sacrifice which would go on for a thousand years. At the end of the sacrifice, the doors of heaven would fling themselves open and Nimi would be welcomed by all the gods into the splendid world where no one grew old and weak or died.

In order to conduct such an important yagna, the king needed to find a great sage to perform it. After much thought, the king decided on Sage Vashishta.

However Vashishta was busy. He scratched his beard thoughtfully and spoke in a quiet voice, 'I would very much like to conduct the sacrifice for you, King Nimi. But I have already allotted the next five hundred years of my time to Indra, the king of gods. So I will be free only after that.'

King Nimi was very disappointed. But he hid his disappointment and said, 'I will wait until you are free. The sacrifice will not be perfect unless you conduct it.'

As the days passed and became years, King Nimi became impatient. Five hundred years seemed too long a time and he couldn't bear to wait any more. One day, he approached Sage Gautama and pleaded with him to officiate at the sacrifice. The sage agreed.

The preparations for the sacrifice began. Forests were cut down for firewood. All the cows in the kingdom were sent to the palace so that there would be adequate milk and ghee. Herbs were gathered in bundles and arranged in rows. Thousands of people gathered in Mithila to witness the great yagna.

The sacrificial fire was lit and huge billows of aromatic smoke blew up into the skies. Up in heaven, Vashishta felt the heat of the flames singe his eyes. He realized that King Nimi had begun the sacrifice without waiting for him.

Vashishta felt anger build within him like monsoon clouds turning the blue skies a dark grey and he rushed to the sacrificial spot.

King Nimi saw Vashishta arrive and hurried to welcome him. But Vashishta ignored the welcoming words and glared at the king. When he saw everyone gathered there and the extent of preparations, he grew even more furious and cursed King Nimi. 'King Nimi, how dare you have someone else perform the sacrifice? How could you have been arrogant? It is your pride that has made you so arrogant . . . the pride that comes from being a powerful emperor. What is an emperor without a body? I curse that you lose this body that houses your insolence and pride!'

King Nimi heard the curse and felt his heart sink. He fell on his knees and pleaded with the sage, 'Please forgive me. I never intended to insult you . . . Ple . . . ple . . . please take back the curse.'

But Vashishta was still angry and began to walk away. King Nimi was now angered by the sage's behaviour and cursed Vashishta, 'Just as I will lose my body because of your curse, you too shall lose your body because of your arrogance that you are a great sage!'

Both the king and the sage were great and righteous souls. So their curses would always be fulfilled. Nimi and Vashishta lost their bodies. The grand yagna was

abandoned and confusion reigned in Mithila. What should have been a day of celebration turned into a day of mourning.

The god of day, Mithra, and the god of night and water, Varuna, decided to step in and resolve the mess. They fashioned a new body for Vashishta and his soul began to dwell in it once again.

King Nimi's body was preserved from decay and it remained intact as if he were immortal. The gods wanted Nimi to return to his body and they said they would relieve him of the curse. But King Nimi declined. He said, 'I know the anguish of being separated from one's body. I do not ever want to go through that distress again.'

So the gods decided that Nimi would be a part of the eyes of all living creatures. And that was how Nimisha, the blink of an eye, came to be.

How the Island of Sri Lanka Came to Be

Mount Sumeru was the tallest mountain in the world. It rose into the clouds farther than the eye could see. Its slopes and terraces were the abode of various gods. Around its majestic form, the stars revolved.

One day, the sage Narada got into an argument with Mount Sumeru on who was more important. 'Look at you,' the mountain mocked. 'You are just a sage. And I am the most important and tallest mountain. Even the sun, moon and stars revolve around me. As for the gods, even they choose to live on me.'

Narada walked away in a huff. But he wasn't going to let the insult pass. So he hit upon a plan. He went to Vayu, the god of wind, and said, 'Do you know what I heard the other day? The mountain Sumeru said there is no one more powerful than him. I said that was true except when it came to you. I said Vayu has the power to shake even you up. But he laughed . . .'

Vayu heard Narada's words and felt a great anger. 'How dare that mountain speak like that? I will have to show him who is more powerful!'

'Do that,' Narada said. 'Break his summit and he will be humbled forever.'

Mount Sumeru heard about Narada's mischief and prayed to Vishnu to protect him. Vishnu sent his bird, the mighty Garuda, to Mount Sumeru. Garuda shielded the mountain with his wings. Each time Vayu hurled forth a great blast of wind, he took the brunt of its force on his body. Vayu tried for many days, but he was unable to even ruffle a leaf on Mount Sumeru while Garuda protected him.

'What shall I do?' Vayu asked Narada. 'This is an unequal contest. As long as Garuda protects him, I cannot even send a little pebble rolling down his side.'

Narada thought for a while and said, 'I will think of a way to lure Garuda away. That will be your chance to show the mountain who is more powerful.'

So Narada pretended to be a devotee in distress and called out, 'Narayana, Narayana, help me!'

Garuda heard someone call his master's name and waited for Vishnu to go to him. But Vishnu didn't and Garuda couldn't bear to hear the cries any more. So he went in search of the man who was seeking help in such desperation.

As soon as Garuda left, Vayu blew several huge gusts of wind at Sumeru. So powerful were the gusts that the top of the mountain was torn off. It fell into the sea and became an island. Today, it is known as Sri Lanka.

How Pushan Became Toothless

Daksha was a mighty king and a sage. He was born from the right thumb of Brahma. His wife Aditi was born from Brahma's left thumb. They had several daughters.

One of the daughters was called Sati. She fell in love with Shiva and wanted to marry him. However, Daksha disapproved of her choice and decreed that she should never meet Shiva again. But Sati had made up her mind and she married Shiva. Daksha was so angry by his daughter's disobedience that he forbade her from entering his home again.

Some time later Daksha decided to conduct a major sacrifice to propitiate Vishnu. All the gods and sages were invited. But he refused to invite either his daughter Sati or her husband Shiva.

Sati was upset by this but she decided to go for the sacrifice. She asked Shiva to go with her. But he refused. 'Don't you have any shame? How can you go to a place where you have not been invited?' he demanded of her.

But Sati shook her head and said, 'I am sure it is a mistake. My father must have meant to send word to us. Besides, why do I need an invitation to go to my father's home?'

When Sati reached Daksha's palace, her father refused to let her enter. 'How dare you show your face here?' he snarled. 'I haven't invited you or your husband. Why have you come?'

'Father,' Sati began.

'Don't call me father. I am not your father. I don't want to see you. Leave this place right now,' he ordered.

The assembled gods and sages watched, aghast. Why was Daksha behaving like this, they wondered. Had he forgotten the might of Shiva's wrath? But Daksha was in no mood to listen to reason.

Humiliated and weeping, Sati returned to her husband. But Shiva wouldn't let her into their home. 'You chose to go to your father's house despite my asking you not to. Now you have no place in my home,' he said coldly.

Sati pleaded for forgiveness but Shiva was much too angry to listen to her. In sorrow and desperation, Sati leapt into a fire and killed herself.

Hearing of her death, Shiva was deeply grieved. He had loved her very much. He sat and mourned her absence, and then started thinking of the manner of her death. He thought of how Daksha, his father-in-law, had insulted both him and Sati. He thought of how it had led him and Sati to quarrel. He thought of how Sati had killed herself. And as he thought of all this, his rage and grief reached a breaking point.

Shiva stormed off to Daksha's palace, where the yagna still continued. In his wrath and deep sorrow, he lost all control of himself. How could they conduct a yagna when his wife had killed herself because of it?

Indra was knocked down flat on his back. Yama's staff was broken into bits. The goddess Saraswati lost her nose and Mithra, the god of day, had his eyes gouged out.

Bhrigu's beard was ripped out and others were stabbed, trampled and even sat upon. As for Pushan, the god and nourisher of cattle, Shiva clenched his fingers into a fist and punched his teeth down his throat. Finally Daksha was decapitated and his head thrown into the fire and only then was Shiva's anger spent.

Amidst the ruins of the yagna, all the gods fell at Shiva's feet and begged for mercy. Now calm once again, Shiva restored them their lost or ruined body parts. However, Daksha's head couldn't be found and so it was replaced with a ram's.

As Pushan had swallowed his own teeth, he had to remain toothless. Since that day, worshippers offer only gruel and cooked ground food when they pray to Pushan.

How Taraka Became Indestructible

The moment Taraka was born, jackals howled, donkeys brayed, the skies darkened and owls hooted. All the people on the earth looked at each other in fear and asked, 'What calamity is going to come upon us?'

Then a wise man said, 'Vajranga, an asura whose name means limbs of diamond, has had a son who is going to wreak much havoc in this world.'

When Taraka grew up, he decided to perform a thousand years of penance to acquire strength and invincibility. He patiently performed the most demanding of austerities. For a hundred years, he stood on one toe with his arms raised and prayed. For another hundred years, he sat in the middle of a ring of fire. For another hundred years, he stood on his hands on a bare rock in the middle of a desert. The gods began to worry that his prayers would make him indestructible and rushed to Brahma to intervene.

So Brahma appeared before Taraka and asked him to put an end to his penance. 'You have proved how strong your will is. Now ask me for what you want,' he said.

Taraka said, 'I want to be invincible.'

'That is an impossible boon. I can't grant you this boon till you set a timeframe to it. You have to say something like "invincible for a thousand years", or some such period.'

Taraka thought for a while. With a sneer he said, 'All right. I will stop my penance if you agree to give me a boon that no one should be able to defeat me except a son born to Shiva.'

Brahma stared at him in shock. Everyone knew that Sati was dead and Shiva didn't have a wife. So how would he have a son? But Brahma knew he was trapped and had to grant Taraka his wish.

As soon as he had obtained the boon, Taraka shed his ascetic clothes and began to rule Sonitapura. He was so powerful that he tyrannized both heaven and earth. He killed, looted, plundered, abducted women and stole anything that caught his eye. From Indra, he snatched his white elephant, Airavata; from the rishis, he took away Kamadhenu, the cow that yielded whatever one desired; he stole the sun god's horses. There was no end to his crimes and all that the gods could do was watch, while Taraka continued his reign of terror, secure in his indestructibility.

What Taraka didn't realize as he went about his reign of terror was that Shakti, Shiva's consort who had been born as Sati first, had been born again as Parvati, the daughter of Himavat, the lord of the Himalayas. As a young girl, she had accompanied her father when he went to pay his respects to Shiva who was meditating in Kailasha. Shiva saw the beautiful girl and rebuked Himavat, 'Do not bring any woman here. I do not want anyone or anything distracting me.'

Parvati had already lost her heart to Shiva. So she stayed behind and tried to win his love with her beauty. But Shiva remained unmoved. So she began praying. Impressed by her devotion, Shiva relented and appeared before her in disguise. As he spoke to Parvati, Shiva realized the extent of her admiration and deep love for him. Suddenly he felt a great love for her swamp him. So he shed his disguise and smiled at her.

And soon, to everyone's delight, they were married. For from this marriage would be born Taraka's destroyer.

How Ganesha Got His Elephant Head

Every day, before she bathed, Parvati applied sandalwood paste and cream to her body. When it was almost dry, she would peel the paste off.

One day, Parvati decided to make something from the peeled-off paste to amuse herself. She created a little man. She liked her handiwork so much that she breathed life into it.

'Son,' she said, 'go, stand by the door and guard it. Do not let anyone in unless I ask you to. I do not want to be disturbed while I am bathing.'

So the little man went to stand by the door.

A little later, Shiva's attendants came to announce that Shiva was on his way and that they would like to prepare the room in readiness for his arrival. But the little man wouldn't let them in. When Shiva reached the palace, he discovered his attendants standing outside, wringing their hands. 'There is this little man inside. But he only looks little. He is so powerful that he threw us all out,' they cried.

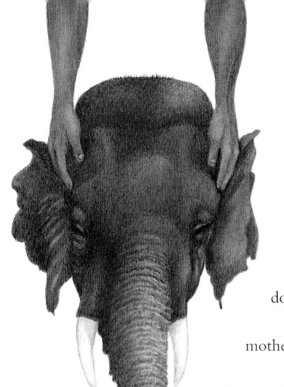

'Who is this creature? How dare he? Doesn't he know who I am?' Shiva said in a loud voice and rushed inside. But the little man wouldn't let Shiva enter the inner rooms either.

'My mother is having a bath. And she said she is not to be disturbed,' he said.

'Your mother! How is it I have a son and don't even know of it?' Shiva mocked.

'I didn't say I was your son. But she is my mother.'

Shiva was so angry with the little man's words that he raised his trident and hurled it and the little man was decapitated. Just then Parvati emerged from her bath. She was very upset to hear of what had happened and began to wail loudly. She took the headless little man and held him close to her. 'How could you do this to him? He is blameless. He was merely obeying my orders. How will sons ever listen to their mothers if fathers keep contradicting orders?' she cried.

Shiva began to feel guilty. Perhaps he had acted too impulsively. To pacify Parvati, he said, 'Don't worry. Your son is mine too. I'll make this all right.'

He called his attendants and asked them to bring the head of the first living creature they encountered.

As the attendants stepped out of the palace, the first creature they saw was a tusker. They brought his head back to Shiva.

The little man was given the elephant's head and brought back to life again. And that was how Ganesha came to be the elephant-headed god.

Ganesha now had both father and mother, and he did his best to be a loving and dutiful son. One day, while Shiva was asleep, he had a visitor: a very powerful sage called Parasurama. Parasurama wanted an audience with Shiva. But Ganesha wouldn't let him in. 'You will have to either wait or come back later. I will not allow you to disturb my father,' he said.

'I'm not paying a social visit. I have something very important to discuss with him,' Parasurama said. 'It has to be said now and can't wait.'

But Ganesha shook his head and wouldn't let Parasurama go past the door.

Parasurama, who had a very short temper, decided to teach the elephant-headed god a lesson and raised his axe. As soon as Ganesha saw the axe, he knew that it was his father's, which meant here was an important visitor, someone Shiva wouldn't mind waking up for. 'Wait,' he cried. 'I will wake up my father . . .'

But Parasurama had already swung his axe and Ganesha took the impact of the blow on his tusk and that was how Ganesha lost one of his tusks.

How Taraka Was Destroyed

Soon Shiva and Parvati had a son of their own. The six-faced Subramanya who rode on a peacock.

Shiva, Parvati and their sons Ganesha, the elephant-headed god, and Subramanya lived very happily in their mountain abode. Meanwhile the gods were getting restless waiting for Subramanya to destroy Taraka. However, there were no signs to indicate that Subramanya was ever going to leave home.

So they turned to Narada for help.

Narada arrived at Kailasha with a wondrous fruit. 'My lord Shiva, I found this fruit of knowledge on my travels and thought that your children should have it.'

Shiva realized that there was some mischief hidden in this and sighed, 'Why have you brought this to me?'

Narada smiled and said, 'This fruit cannot be divided and has to be eaten by one person alone. Whoever eats it will become the wisest being of all. So I thought that you would be the best one to decide who is worthy of it. Here it is,' he said, offering the fruit.

When Narada left, both the children began clamouring for the fruit that glowed a golden yellow and was said to be marvellously sweet.

Shiva didn't know what to do. How could he choose between his sons? So he came up with an idea. 'Since there is only one fruit, I will have to make it a contest. The one who wins will get the fruit.'

Parvati began to look worried and she said, 'I don't like this. One of them is going to get hurt.'

'No, Mother. We know that only one person can have it. We'd like a contest,' the boys said. 'We agree!'

'In that case,' Shiva said, 'the one who circles the world and comes back first gets the fruit.'

Subramanya smiled and set forth on his peacock. He knew his peacock was swift and no one would be able to beat him, especially not Ganesha who rode on a rat.

But when Subramanya returned triumphantly, he found to his shock and dismay that Ganesha was already back. 'What is this?' he demanded. 'How did you circle the world and come back so quickly?'

Ganesha smiled. 'My world is my parents. It takes no time to circle them. See . . .' he said and made a full circle of his parents again.

Shiva and Parvati smiled. 'He is right, you know. So he gets the fruit!'

But Subramanya felt cheated. 'This is not fair. This is a trick, a wordplay, and I don't accept this.'

Shiva and Parvati tried to persuade him to accept the decision but Subramanya stormed from there in a huff. On his way, he bumped into Taraka. The asura saw the peacock Subramanya rode on and wanted to add it to his menagerie of wondrous animals—Airavata the white elephant, Kamadhenu the cow, and the sun god's horses. So he tried to wrest the peacock away. Subramanya, who was already angry with the world, grew even more furious at Taraka's effrontery. How dare he, he thought, and glared at Taraka. 'Do you think I am going to let everyone walk over me? It is time someone taught you a lesson!'

Thus began a great battle and Taraka was defeated and destroyed.

That was how Brahma's boon that only Shiva's son could kill Taraka was fulfilled.

What Aurva Did with His Rage

There was a king named Kritavirya who was very generous to the priests in his kingdom. The priests were known as Bhrigus, because all of them were descendants of the sage Bhargava. Such was his generosity that the Bhrigus grew very rich while the royal treasury was almost emptied out.

After Kritavirya's death, his sons and grandsons discovered that they would soon have to go out with a begging bowl and beg for food. They appealed to the Bhrigus to help them make ends meet till such time as they recouped their fortunes.

However, the priests turned their heads away and said, 'Do not look to us for help. We have very little money ourselves.'

'But how can that be?' the descendants of Kritavirya demanded. 'We know that our father emptied out the royal treasury for you. Where did it all go?'

'Once you make a gift of something to someone, it's none of your business what they do with it,' the Bhrigus said angrily.

The descendants of Kritavirya looked at each other. What were they to do now? Some of the priests, they heard, had buried their fortune.

'There is nothing else we can do but kill them,' one of them said.

'Yes, that's right,' another said.

'We did ask them to help us. But they refused. And as kshatriyas, it is our duty to battle for what is ours,' another added.

The sons and grandsons of Kritavirya set out to slay every one of the Bhrigus. No one was spared, not even children in the womb. One woman, however, concealed her unborn child in a secret place.

When the kshatriyas returned to their palace, a spy came to them, 'Your Majesties, one of the Bhrigus is still alive. It lives in its mother's thigh.'

The descendants of Kritavirya rushed to destroy that child. Just as they arrived at his mother's house, the boy burst out of his mother's thigh. So bright was his radiance that the kshatriyas were blinded and the child managed to escape. As he was born from the thigh (*uru*), he was known as Aurva.

Aurva lived in the forest. He wanted to destroy all the kshatriyas, and so he performed terrifying penances to secure great powers. Even the gods were alarmed at what the young man was doing. But before they could intervene, something else happened.

One night, Aurva had a dream where his forefathers appeared to him. They said, 'We understand your anger but it does not befit someone as righteous as you to expend so much energy on anger. Instead, use it to save the helpless and needy.'

Aurva woke up and resolved that he would no longer carry forth his anger. Just as he had emerged from the thigh, he produced from his own thigh the fire of his rage. He threw this into the sea where it became a being called Haya-siras, which had the face of a horse.

So great was the fury of the fire that Haya-siras cried, 'I am hungry; let me consume the world.' Soon, he destroyed many parts of the world with his flames.

Finally, Brahma appeared before Haya-siras and promised him a home where he would be happy. This was at the mouth of the ocean. Since then, submarine fires are called Aurva.

One of Aurva's sons was Richika, whose son was Jamad-Agni. And it was Jamad-Agni who was Parasurama's father.

How the Sons of Sagara Were Born

Bahu, the king of Ayodhya, was driven out of his kingdom by the Haihayas, a barbaric tribe. He took refuge in the forest with his wives. One of them soon discovered that she was pregnant but another wife was so jealous that she fed the pregnant queen a drug to prevent her from delivering the baby.

And so the baby remained in the womb for seven years.

Before the seven years were up, Bahu died. The pregnant queen wanted to join her husband on the funeral pyre. Just then, the sage Aurva arrived. He persuaded her not to do that. He said, 'Your child will be born soon and he will be a great and noble king.'

The queen gave birth to the baby and Aurva named the child Sagara, meaning, with poison. Sagara grew up hearing tales of what happened to Bahu. He was determined to exterminate the Haihayas and win back his kingdom.

When he grew older, Aurva gave Sagara the agneyastra, a celestial fire weapon. Armed with this, Sagara defeated the Haihayas and regained his throne.

Not satisfied yet, Sagara decided to rid the world of the various barbaric tribes—the Yavanas, Sakas, Paradas, Pahlavas and Haihayas. But his family priest Vashishta asked Sagara to spare them. However, Sagara was not going to let them get away unpunished. So he said, 'Holy Sage Vashishta, I cannot disobey your words but I will impose certain conditions on them if they wish to be spared.'

The barbarians agreed, thinking anything was better than facing death.

So the Yavanas were asked to shave their heads completely. The Sakas had to shave the upper half of their heads. The Paradas had to let their hair grow long as a woman's and the Pahlavas had to let their beards grow.

Sagara had two wives called Sumati and Kesini. When, after many years of marriage, he didn't have any children, he appealed to the sage Aurva for help. Aurva smiled and said, 'Your one wife will have one son and the other sixty thousand sons. Let them choose who will have how many.'

Kesini chose to have one son, and Sumati was given the boon of sixty thousand sons.

In time, each woman delivered. Kesini gave birth to a boy who was named Asamanjas. Sumati gave birth to a gourd containing sixty thousand seeds. Sagara placed these seeds in little bowls of milk. Ten months later, each seed turned into a baby boy.

And that is how Sagara came to have sixty thousand and one sons.

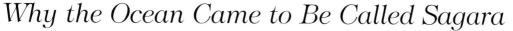

Why the Ocean Came to Be Called Sagara

As long as the boys were young, King Sagara and his queens were happy. But as they started growing up, their troubles began.

Asamanjas grew to become wild and wicked. Finally, Sagara was so angry with him that he disowned the boy.

Sumati's sixty thousand sons were no better. But they were too many in number, almost the size of an army. How could Sagara send so many of them away? Besides, he was frightened of what havoc they would cause if left to their own devices. So he kept them in his kingdom and found them numerous tasks to keep them out of trouble.

One day Sagara decided to conduct an Ashwamedha sacrifice to establish his sovereignty over the entire empire. He called his sixty thousand sons and said, 'It is most important that nothing happens to the sacrificial horse. I would like you to guard the horse.'

The sons agreed and diligently watched over the horse. But one night, the horse disappeared.

'Father,' they cried, rushing to the king, 'it can be no ordinary person who stole the horse. There were sixty thousand of us and who would dare come against us?'

The king nodded and said, 'I know for sure the horse is not on the earth nor is it in heaven. That leaves just the netherworld. Perhaps it is somewhere there.'

So the sons began to dig deep into the infernal regions and when they had dug deep and wide, they entered the netherworld where they found the horse grazing. They saw Sage Kapila was seated close by, meditating. 'He must be the thief,' they said amongst themselves. 'Look at him. He thinks no one will find out that he stole our horse.'

'Chop his head off,' one said.

'Spike him with a spear,' suggested another.

'Club him to death,' a third added.

Suddenly the sage opened his eyes. At one glance, he understood what Sagara's sons were planning. He opened his eyes wide in anger. The flame of his wrath was so powerful that they were all burnt to ashes.

On earth, Sagara waited and waited for his sons to return. Finally, he despatched Ansumat, Asamanjas's son, to look for his uncles.

When Ansumat reached the underworld, he soon discovered the remains of his uncles. The air was filled with their groans and moans as they pleaded to be released from this torment.

'Your Holiness,' Ansumat appealed to the sage Kapila, 'please forgive my uncles and restore their bodies. I wish to perform the ceremonies that will ensure their passage to the other world.'

The sage looked at the young man. After a while he spoke, 'They will ascend to the other world only if you bring down the river of heaven to the earth. Meanwhile, take this horse and return to your grandfather.'

Ansumat returned with the horse and the sacrifice was completed.

But Sagara was much too troubled to rest in peace. 'I had sixty thousand and one sons and none are by my side now,' he thought. So deep was his sorrow that his tears filled the chasm his sons had dug and became an ocean. Since then, the ocean has been known as Sagara.

Why Ganga Came to Earth

After King Sagara's death, his son Asamanjas succeeded to the throne. He was a reformed man and forgot all his wild ways. He was succeeded by his son Ansumat, who was succeeded by his son Dilipa. However, even though several generations had passed, Sagara's sixty thousand sons were still not released from their torment.

When Dilipa's son Bhagirath came to the throne, his great-uncles began to appear in his dreams. 'Help us! Free us! Save us!' they begged and pleaded. Soon, he began to hear them in his waking hours too. Everywhere that Bhagirath went, he was followed by their cries.

Finally, Bhagirath decided to try to save Sagara's sons. He knew from his grandfather that in order to do so he would have to bring the river of heaven to the earth.

Bhagirath began a series of penances. Such were his austerities that Vishnu was moved. He told the goddess Ganga, who flowed from his toe, that she would have to go with Bhagirath and flow down to the earth.

Ganga had no option; she had to follow Bhagirath. But she was enraged at having to descend to the earth. Such was her rage that she gushed down with a huge force that would have smashed the earth to bits.

But, on Bhagirath's plea, Shiva stood in the path of her torrential waters and bore the brunt of her might on his head. He tied her down with his matted locks until her anger had passed and she had broken into seven more gentle rivers. These became the seven holy rivers, known as the sapta-sindhuva. Thus Ganga reached the earth.

Bhagirath led Ganga across the earth and to the sea and then on to the underworld, where Sagara's sons dwelled in eternal torment. Her waters spread over their ashes. The souls of the sixty thousand brothers were purified and they were finally allowed entry to the other world.

Since Bhagirath brought her down to the earth, Ganga is sometimes also known as Bhagirathi.

He Who Strikes with the Axe
Vishnu's Sixth Avatar—Parasurama

Jamad-Agni was born to Richika, a brahmin. From his mother, who was a kshatriya and of the warrior clan by birth, Jamad-Agni inherited a natural aptitude for the skills of warfare and mastered it. And from his father, Jamad-Agni learned all the holy lore. When he was an adult, he made the forest his home just as his father had.

In time Jamad-Agni decided to marry, and he chose Renuka who was a princess. Renuka took to life in the hermitage as though she had been born to it and they lived very happily. Soon five children were born to them and there was nothing more Renuka desired.

One day when Renuka went to the river to fetch water, she saw King Chitraratha and his wife sitting side by side, caressing each other and whispering endearments. Renuka watched them with envy, wondering why it was that her husband never looked at her just as Chitraratha had gazed at his wife. Stifling a sigh, Renuka returned to the hermitage but Jamad-Agni perceived the change in her. He was so angry with her for having doubted his love that he called out to his children, 'My sons, come here.'

One by one, all five sons came to stand by their father. 'Your mother is no longer who she was when she woke up this morning. She has fallen from grace and I do not want her here or alive. I order you to kill her.'

The sons looked at their father in shock. What was wrong with him? Rumanwat, Sushena, Vasu and Viswavasu, the four elder sons, shook their heads, 'We refuse to do any such thing. How can you ask us to murder our mother?' they cried.

Jamad-Agni stared at them furiously. 'How dare you disobey me? Since you stand there shaking your heads like idiots, that's what you will be. I curse you to turn into idiots.'

'What about you?' he asked, turning to the fifth son.

The fifth son was an avatar of Vishnu.

Now at that time, the world was being tyrannized by the kshatriyas and every day thousands were killed, maimed or punished for no fault of theirs. Kartavirya, their king, had obtained the boon of a thousand arms, a golden chariot that went wherever he willed it to go, invincibility and death at the hands of a man known to the whole world. He was so powerful that he once went to Lanka and took its king Ravana as his prisoner. However, he let the asura king go once Ravana acknowledged his greatness. With this knowledge his arrogance grew hundredfold and he did as he pleased. His clan too became nastier than ever. In grief, the people of the world turned to Vishnu and pleaded, 'There is no more goodness left on this earth. Save us from death at the hands of these merciless rulers!'

So a son was born to Jamad-Agni, and even as a young lad, he performed such severe austerities that Shiva appeared before him and taught him the use of arms. As his personal weapon, Shiva gave him an axe which once raised would rest only when it had destroyed his opponent. Henceforth, the fifth son of Jamad-Agni was known as Parasurama or Rama with the axe.

When Parasurama heard his father's orders, without speaking a word he raised his axe and chopped his mother's head off from her neck. Jamad-Agni beamed at his son and said, 'I am pleased with you. Ask me a boon and I shall give it to you.' Parasurama bent his head and said, 'In that case, Father, please restore my mother to life and my brothers back to their senses.'

Jamad-Agni did as Parasurama asked him to.

Some time later when Parasurama, his brothers and their father were away, Kartavirya visited the hermitage. Renuka welcomed the king and entertained him as well as she could. But the king repaid the hospitality by taking away the sacrificial calf. When Parasurama returned, he found his mother in tears. 'Your father is going to blame me for this. As it is, he finds fault with everything I do! What shall I do? I told the king what he was doing was wrong, but he wouldn't listen to me.'

'Don't worry, Mother,' Parasurama said. 'I shall settle this with the king.'

So Parasurama went looking for Kartavirya. 'Your tenure has come to an end,' Parasurama hollered. 'Never again will you oppress harmless folks. Never again will you rule the world with fear.'

With his axe, Parasurama cut off all the thousand arms of Kartavirya and then killed him.

Parasurama's anger could turn the world to ashes and he now retired to a forest to meditate and calm his agitated mind. While he was in the forest, Kartavirya's sons came to the hermitage and killed Jamad-Agni to avenge their father's death.

Now Parasurama's anger could no longer be checked and he took an oath to cleanse the world of these demon-like kshatriyas. Twenty-one times he went around the world killing all the kshatriyas and he filled five large lakes with their blood.

Then, content that his work had been done, he went to the western coast of the land and flung his axe into the ocean. From the waters there emerged a thin strip of land which Varuna gave him as a gift, and that was how Kerala was formed.

How Indra Prevented Drought

Ahi was a demon who hated the gods more than anything in the whole world. He constantly sought ways to trouble them and, in return, was always being punished by them. But with every defeat, his anger grew and he swore to destroy the gods and all life on the earth as well.

Sometimes he took the form of a mammoth serpent and troubled the world by drinking deep of all the waters that were available. So he was also known as Vritra or the serpent of drought. When that happened, Indra would have to come to the rescue by sending rain and filling the lakes and rivers with water again.

Once, when all the gods were away attending a celestial sacrifice, Ahi decided to teach them a lesson for not inviting him. He swallowed all the cosmic waters and then coiled around a mountain range.

When the gods returned to find the cosmic waters gone, they instantly knew who the culprit was.

They turned to Indra in desperation to help them retrieve the cosmic waters and Indra set forth to look for the serpent of drought. Indra rode on his white elephant, Airavata; in his right hand he carried a thunderbolt and in his left hand arrows, a great hook and a net to entangle his foe.

Soon Indra spotted a giant serpent coiled around a mountain range and he knew he had found the enemy. Indra shot a few arrows but the arrows struck the serpent's armour-like scales and fell bent and broken. Then he tried to entangle the serpent but the serpent was much too big.

Indra retreated for a while to think. He knew that he had only one weapon left and it would have to be used carefully. For with each use, the power of the weapon would weaken. Where could Ahi have hidden the cosmic waters? He looked carefully

and saw that Ahi had sheltered both its head and tail. Is that where the waters are hidden, Indra wondered. If so, where should he strike?

Suddenly Indra knew that Ahi intended to trick him. So with a smile, Indra hurled his thunderbolt at the stomach of the serpent. The thunderbolt was a deadly weapon and it split the serpent's stomach, releasing the waters and generating life. From then on, Indra was worshipped every time drought struck the land.

Why Indra Is Also Known as Sahasraksha

Ahalya was the most beautiful woman on earth. She was created by Brahma and given in marriage to Sage Gautama.

One day, Indra saw Ahalya. 'Who is she?' he wondered. 'I have never seen a woman so beautiful.'

Indra found out that she was Gautama's wife. But he was so smitten by her beauty that he did not care. He realized that Ahalya loved her husband and would never look at another man. So Indra asked the moon to help him deceive Ahalya.

One night, the moon turned itself into a cock and crowed at midnight. Gautama heard the cock's crow and assumed that it was time to wake up. He left his room, went outside and began to prepare for his morning prayers. While he was gone, Indra took the form of the sage and went to Ahalya's bed.

When Gautama discovered what had happened, he was so enraged that he

expelled Ahalya from the hermitage. He said that she would no longer be the most beautiful woman on earth. Instead, she would become invisible.

Ahalya fell at his feet and begged his forgiveness. She said she too had been deceived by Indra.

The sage relented at her sorrow. He said that she would not become invisible, but she would be turned into a rock. When Vishnu, in his avatar as Rama, stepped on her, she would be free.

Gautama then turned to Indra and it was on him that he unleashed his fury. He cursed Indra that a thousand marks would appear on his skin. Everywhere he went, when people saw those marks, they would know what a cheat he was.

Stricken by remorse, Indra too begged forgiveness. Gautama, who was a very kind man, relented. The marks were turned into eyes and that was how Indra came to be known as Sahasraksha or the thousand-eyed one.

But the story didn't end there.

Around the time Ahalya was freed from her curse and was reconciled with her husband, Ravana, the lord of Lanka, went into Indra's kingdom and waged a fierce battle. Ravana's son Meghanada had been granted the boon of making himself invisible when he chose to. Invoking this boon, he fought against Indra and defeated him. Meghanada took Indra back to Lanka as his prisoner. As a result of this victory, Meghanada came to be known as Indrajit, or the one who defeated Indra.

Brahma and the other gods approached Ravana and asked them to release Indra. Ravana laughed, 'Why should I let him go? He is a prisoner of war. As long as he is here, everyone will know that no one can vanquish me.'

'Everyone knows that no one can defeat you,' Brahma pleaded. 'Please let him go.'

Indrajit went to his father's side and whispered something in his ear. Ravana listened to him and then slapped his thigh and laughed. Turning to the gods he said, 'I will let Indra go on one condition. Grant my son the boon of immortality and you can have Indra back.'

The gods looked at one another, perplexed and troubled. Indrajit had already proved what a great warrior he was. To make him immortal would make him invincible.

Brahma said, 'I cannot grant you this boon for all perpetuity. Instead, I shall grant Indrajit immortality on the battlefield.'

The father and son looked at each other and smiled. No one would dare come near Indrajit except when surrounded by an army. It was the best they could get, they knew. And so Indra was released.

On the way back, Indra sat humiliated and downcast in the chariot. Brahma looked at him and said, 'Do not look so sad. This humiliation is your punishment for having cheated the sage Gautama. I hope this will teach you never to desire another man's wife.'

From then on, Indra concentrated all his powers on helping the world.

How the Kingdom of Anga Was Saved

Once, the kingdom of Anga was affected by a severe drought. Crops withered because there was no rain and people died for lack of food. No matter what the king Romapada did, the rains wouldn't come. Finally he beseeched the holy men in his kingdom, 'There must be something we can do to make the rains fall. My subjects' suffering gets harder for me to bear each day.'

The holy men thought for a while and said, 'There is a young sage called Rishyasringa. Invite him to our kingdom. He brings rain and plenty with him wherever he goes.'

Rishyasringa was the son of Vibhandaka. Since his mother was a doe, he was born with a little horn on his forehead. He had been brought up in the forest by his father and had seen no other human being yet even though he was a young man.

The king knew that if he invited the young sage, his father would prevent him from leaving the forest. So Rishyasringa would have to be tricked into coming to the kingdom. He discussed this with his courtiers and they decided to send the most beautiful dancer in their kingdom, Lalita, to the forest.

The dancer made a beautiful garden on a boat and, in its middle, had a small hermitage built. Then the boat sailed down the river till it got close to Vibhandaka's hermitage.

Trying not to let her fear show, the dancer went to the hermitage. Fortunately, the older sage was away. Rishyasringa was bewitched by this young and beautiful woman. He thought she was a young sage like him.

'Who are you?' he asked, and then, unable to

stop himself, he touched her hair and skin and said, 'Your skin is so smooth and your hair is so black. Father's skin is all wrinkled and his hair is grey.'

The dancer smiled and said, 'In my hermitage, there are others like me. We eat the most delicious of fruits and our songs will fill you with great happiness. Wouldn't you like to visit our hermitage?'

Rishyasringa was captivated by her description and allowed himself to be lured into the boat. He was soon lost in a world of pleasure and didn't realize that they had set sail. When the boat reached the kingdom of Anga, Rishyasringa was received with great respect. The moment he set foot in the land, the rains came and every lake and well, pond and river filled with water. Delighted, the king offered his daughter Shanta to Rishyasringa as his wife. Rishyasringa was enchanted by Shanta's beauty and agreed. He married the princess and stayed on there. Thus he saved the kingdom from further misery.

Meanwhile Vibhandhaka returned to the hermitage and found his son missing. He set out in search of him. The king had anticipated this. So on the road to his kingdom, he had magnificent cattle and other marvellous things lined and he instructed his men to say, no matter who asked, that all of it was the young sage Rishyasringa's possessions.

Vibhandaka was pleased to hear that his son was being taken care of with such attention and, by the time he reached the palace, his anger had lessened. When he saw Rishyasringa and his wife seated together on the throne in complete happiness, his anger evaporated totally. He blessed the couple and left.

Later, when they had enough of the pleasures of the palace, Rishyasringa and Shanta went back to the forest and lived there in peace and happiness.

Why Kala-Nemi Failed to Outwit Hanuman

Kala-Nemi was the uncle of Ravana, the king of Lanka. During the great battle with Rama and his monkey-army, Kala-Nemi made his nephew Ravana an offer. He would kill Hanuman if Ravana would reward him with half the kingdom. Ravana agreed.

Kala-Nemi waited for a suitable moment, and soon his opportunity arrived. An arrow caused Lakshmana a grievous injury and, to save his life, Hanuman went to the Gandha-Madana mountain in search of medicinal herbs.

Kala-Nemi followed him there and, disguised as a hermit, approached Hanuman. 'Son of Vayu,' he said, 'you have blessed this mountain by setting foot on it. Please bless my hermitage too by coming there and sharing a meal with us.'

'I will not touch food until Lakshmana is well. But I shall certainly come to your hermitage,' Hanuman said.

Before entering the hermitage, to cleanse himself, Hanuman went to bathe in a nearby lake.

In the lake lived a wicked crocodile that killed any living creature that entered its

waters. As soon as Hanuman placed his foot in the water, the crocodile seized it. But Hanuman dragged the creature out and killed it. From the dead body of the crocodile, a lovely apsara emerged. She folded her hands and bowed before Hanuman.

'You have freed me,' she said. 'I was cursed by Daksha to be a crocodile till you would come here to save me. And now it is my turn to save you. Beware of the hermit who has invited you to his home. He is none other than Kala-Nemi, Ravana's uncle.'

Hanuman smiled and went to the hermitage. Kala-Nemi rushed to greet him. 'You have honoured this little hermitage,' he said in a voice full of piety.

Before he could say another word, Hanuman grabbed the hermit by his beard and raised him off the ground. 'Did you think I wouldn't find out who you are?'

Kala-Nemi struggled to escape but Hanuman held him in a vice-like grip. 'Your presence on this mountain will make it impure,' said the monkey-lord. 'Go back to where you belong.'

Hanuman grabbed Kala-Nemi's feet and whirled him around his head. Then he flung him as hard as he could throw.

Kala-Nemi went flying through the air and landed at the foot of Ravana's throne, dead. And so ended Kala-Nemi's hopes of owning half of Lanka.

How Bali Was Defeated

Kiskindhya was a kingdom in the southern part of India. It was ruled by Bali, the monkey-king, whose father was Indra, the king of gods. When Bali was very young, his father was so pleased by his conduct that he gave him a boon. Indra blessed his son that no matter who battled with Bali, the opponent's powers would be reduced by half and the powers would shift to Bali during the time of the battle.

Soon no one could vanquish Bali and he became so very powerful that he defeated Ravana in a wrestling combat.

Once a demon, Dundupi, approached Bali and challenged him to a duel. Furious at the demon's effrontery, Bali decided to teach him a lesson. He began to wrestle with Dundupi. But the demon managed to free himself from Bali's clutches and flee. Bali, not about to let him go, chased the demon into a cave. He stood at the mouth of the cave and called to Sugriva, his younger brother, 'I am going after the demon and when I get him in my hands, I will break every bone in his body. I want you to wait here till

I come back. If milk flows out, you will know that I have succeeded. But if blood flows out, you must leave immediately and protect our families and kinsmen.'

Sugriva waited outside the mouth of the cave. Some time later he heard Bali yelling, 'Help! Help! I'm being killed!' Then, to Sugriva's horror, he saw a rivulet of blood flow out of the cave and knew that his brother had been vanquished. In anger and grief, he rolled a mighty rock and sealed the mouth of the cave. Then he went back to the kingdom and assumed the role of the king.

However, what had really happened was that the demon had realized he was about to die and in his final moments had played a trick. As he struggled, he called out in a voice like Bali's and, when he saw Bali invoke a rivulet of milk, he conjured it to look like blood. Bali was unaware of the trick and set about beating the life out of Dundupi. After Bali killed the demon, he came to the mouth of the cave and found a huge rock blocking his way. He stared at the rock in surprise and then pushed it aside. 'Where are you, Sugriva, my dear brother?' he called. But Sugriva wasn't there. Bali began to get anxious. He rushed to his palace and there he found his brother seated on the throne.

Bali thought his brother Sugriva had wanted to kill him and had sealed the mouth of the cave to ensure that. He stared at his brother angrily. 'So this is what you wanted . . . all this while you were pretending to be a loving brother and in your head you were plotting my downfall. You are a traitor!'

When Sugriva saw his brother alive and well, he rushed towards him joyously. 'I'm so happy to see you. We all thought you were dead!'

'Stop pretending, Sugriva,' Bali roared. 'You mean you thought I was dead! You *wanted* me dead so you could be king. But you shall no longer be king!'

Sugriva tried to explain. 'I never wanted to be king. But the ministers forced me to be one till your son was old enough to be the ruler. Please believe me, my dear brother!'

'Don't call me brother. If you truly were one, you would have waited for me till I returned,' Bali said.

'But I heard you scream that you were being killed and then I saw blood flow out,' Sugriva said.

'Did you think a demon was going to destroy me?' Bali demanded.

And even though all his ministers tried to explain, Bali wouldn't listen. He banished Sugriva from the kingdom and Sugriva went to the forest with a band of his faithful followers, which included Hanuman, the son of Vayu.

Later, when Rama and Lakshmana passed through the forests seeking Sita, they met Sugriva who told them the sad story of his banishment. He narrated how Bali had seized the throne back and, to make matters worse, had married Sugriva's wife, thereby depriving him of his home and family.

'Everything I have is yours. But I have nothing to offer you,' Sugriva told Rama.

'Do not lose heart. I shall ensure that you get justice,' Rama said.

'But no one can defeat Bali. He is so powerful,' Sugriva said. 'Besides, our father's boon ensures that in a battle his opponent's powers will be reduced by half.'

'Listen to me. I have a plan. This will not be a battle in the conventional sense . . .' Rama said.

So Sugriva went to the palace doors and roared, 'Bali, come out! I challenge you to a battle!'

Bali looked up from what he was doing and wondered: 'What is wrong with that fool, Sugriva? Has he gone mad? Does he think he can defeat me?'

'Go away!' Bali screamed.

But Sugriva continued to holler challenges. 'Are you so scared that you are hiding behind the skirts of the women in the palace? Perhaps you too should begin to wear one!' he taunted.

Bali lost his temper and stepped out of the palace and they began to wrestle. Rama, who was hiding behind a tree, shot an arrow which pierced Bali's heart and killed him.

Thus Sugriva became king again and his monkey-army helped Rama in his battle against Ravana.

How Balarama Destroyed Two Mighty Asuras

Once again when the universe was ravaged by evil rakshasa kings and there was no one who could vanquish them, the time came for Vishnu to make his appearance. He took two hairs, one black and one white, and set them afloat. These became the children of Devaki. The dark one was Krishna and the fair one, Balarama. As soon as they were born, they were carried away to Gokula so that their uncle Kansa wouldn't kill them.

King Kansa had deposed his father, Ugrasena, as the ruler of Mathura. One day, he was told that his nephews would destroy him and so he murdered each one of Devaki's children. However, both Balarama and Krishna were smuggled away to Gokula soon after they were born, where Rohini looked after Balarama and Yashodhara, Krishna.

Krishna and Balarama were completely unlike each other not only in looks but in their behaviour too. But that didn't stop them from being the best of friends and together they had many adventures.

Just as Krishna killed many demons, Balarama too had his share of victories. When Balarama was a young boy, an asura tried to carry him off. The asura had disguised himself as a cowherd and so for a while Balarama sat on his shoulders quite happily. 'Where are we going, Uncle?' he asked.

'Your father wanted me to take you to see the new calf which was born yesterday,' the asura said.

Balarama began to feel something was not quite right. He was familiar with every cow and calf in the place and knew that no calf had been born the day before. But he kept quiet. Soon he saw that the asura was walking in the wrong direction from where the cows grazed and he asked, 'Where are you going? This is not the way.'

The asura laughed. 'This is the right way. The way to your death.'

But Balarama was not going to give up without a fight. So he began to beat the demon's head. His hands were so strong that his blows cracked the demon's head and he fell to the ground dead.

Some days later, as Balarama was crossing a narrow bridge, at the other end stood an ass, which refused to budge. It was the great demon Dhenuka in disguise, and his plan was to kick Balarama to death. 'He is a little boy and one kick will be enough,' the demon thought.

Balarama looked at the ass that was blocking his path and said politely, 'I have come all this way. All you need to do is to step a few feet back. Please let me pass.'

Again and again, Balarama appealed to the ass. But the ass brayed and refused to move. So Balarama slapped it on its rump to make it run away. The ass rolled its eyes, snorted and raised its leg to kick Balarama. But the boy was very nimble on his feet and jumped out of the way in time.

Balarama, unlike Krishna, had a quick temper and he lost it now. He also realized that the ass was no ordinary animal. So Balarama seized the ass and began whirling it around by one of its legs till the creature was dead and then he flung the carcass. It landed on a tree and the disguise fell off. Now everyone knew that Balarama had killed the wicked demon Dhenuka.

What Happened When Balarama Wielded the Plough

When Balarama was a young man, he accompanied Krishna to Mathura and helped him destroy Kansa, their wicked uncle.

Away from the simple life of Gokula, both Krishna and Balarama discovered the pleasures of royal living. Balarama developed a fondness for wine and sometimes went on drinking bouts.

Once when Balarama had drunk several glasses of wine, he decided to have a bath. After the attendants prepared the bath, he refused to bathe in the palace and said he would like to bathe in the waters of the Yamuna.

'But, Your Highness, the river is far away and you are in no condition to walk or ride to the riverbank,' the attendants said bewildered.

Balarama lolled back on the cushions and said, 'Why should I go to the river? The river will come here. All I need to do is call it.'

The attendants tried to hide their smiles. 'He is so drunk that he doesn't know what he is saying,' they thought. Balarama saw their smiles and snorted. 'You don't believe me, is that it? Just watch. Yamuna, hey you river, come to me. I would like to bathe in your waters,' he said loudly.

But the river didn't appear. Balarama called again but the river didn't heed his command. Balarama began to get angry. 'How dare you be so . . . so . . .' Balarama spluttered in rage, unable to find words.

He then rose from his seat, grabbed the plough that was his favourite weapon, and stalked to the riverbank. He plunged the plough into the waters and dragged it this way and that. 'You wouldn't come to me. Now you have to go everywhere that I do. Do you understand?' he muttered.

Balarama walked first to the east, then to the south, then to the north and to the west and then again to the north. All the while he held his plough in the water and the river was dragged after him.

The river began to feel dizzy with the constant change in direction. Yamuna assumed a human form and appeared before Balarama, begging for forgiveness. His pride satisfied, Balarama let it go.

There were many times that Balarama wielded his plough to deadly effect. When Duryodhana, the Kaurava prince, kidnapped and imprisoned Balarama's nephew Samba, and kept him as a prisoner, Balarama asked for his release. Duryodhana laughed scornfully and refused. Balarama thrust his plough under the ramparts of Hastinapura and began to shake it. The city trembled and seemed in imminent danger of collapsing, so finally Duryodhana was forced to release Samba.

Dwivida, a demon in the form of a great ape, longed to get his hands on Balarama's plough. With the plough he would be invincible, he thought. So he stole the plough and began to taunt Balarama. 'Let us see how strong you are without your plough.'

Balarama grunted in reply and grabbed the great ape and began whirling it in the air till blood spewed from its eyes, nostrils, ears and mouth. Then he hurled it on to the ground. The ape fell on the crest of a mountain and such was the weight of its body and the force of the throw that the mountain splintered into a hundred pieces.

Meanwhile King Raivata, who had a very beautiful daughter called Revati, was looking for a husband for her. Since she was as strong as she was beautiful, he thought he would have to consult with Brahma on who would be worthy of her. Brahma suggested that he choose Balarama and so King Raivata went to Balarama and gave him Revati as his wife.

Balarama looked at Revati carefully. 'She is very beautiful,' he said, 'but she is much too tall and I don't want my wife to be taller than I am.'

So he shortened her with the end of his plough and then married her. Revati might thus have lost a few inches but she didn't lose her incredible stamina. When she discovered Balarama's fondness for wine, she began to join him in his drinking bouts. That way he didn't get drunk and, since she had a strong head, she was not affected no matter how much she drank. They lived very happily together and had two sons.

How Krishna Taught Indra a Lesson

The people of Vraja, near Mathura, lived off the land. They grazed the cows on the grass that grew abundantly and bathed the cattle in the waters of the Yamuna. The cows produced so much milk and of such wonderful quality that their milk, curds and butter were much sought after. To thank Indra for giving the region plenty of rain, the people of Vraja offered a grand yagna to him every year.

One year, when Krishna was a young lad, he questioned the elders of the community, 'Why do you offer prayers to Indra? It isn't as if he's doing anything extraordinary. It is his business to provide rain.'

'Don't speak like that, Krishna,' they cautioned. 'If Indra gets angry, he'll trouble us with too little rain or too much. Besides, conducting a sacrifice is a tradition. Everyone here has a good time.'

'I'm not saying that we shouldn't conduct a sacrifice. All I'm saying is why do it in honour of Indra?' Krishna said.

'Then who shall we do it for?' the older men asked.

'How about the mountain Govardhan? Don't our cows graze on its slopes? Don't we collect firewood from its trees? Don't we drink the water from its streams? Don't we live on its sides? And have we ever thought of saying thanks to the mountain that is part of our lives in so many ways?' Krishna spoke with a smile.

When Krishna smiled and spoke so sweetly, no one could resist him. That year the sacrifice was conducted in honour of the great mountain Govardhan.

Indra was furious when he found out that the people of Vraja had offered a sacrifice to the mountain instead of him. 'How dare they?' he fumed. 'I'll teach them such a lesson that they will come begging to me and will never dare risk my displeasure.'

So Indra sent a storm towards Vraja and for many days the rain came pouring down. Lightning criss-crossed the skies and thunder rumbled ominously, making

cows low and babies cry and old people take shelter under their beds. Everything was sodden and the level of the river began to rise. Soon it had risen beyond the banks and still the rains didn't stop. 'Let me see what Krishna and his mountain-friend can do to save them,' Indra laughed.

Krishna realized that Indra was punishing the villagers. This angered him and he decided to teach Indra a lesson. 'Come with me,' he said to the villagers. 'I will take you to a place where you will be dry and safe. Indra won't be able to harm you with his rains or thunderbolts.'

Krishna led them to the foot of the mountain Govardhan and asked the mountain for permission to move it. When the mountain agreed, Krishna lifted it with his little finger and beneath it all the villagers huddled together.

For seven days, Krishna held the mountain aloft. Finally, Indra knew there was nothing more to be done. He went to Krishna and offered his homage. 'Forgive me for my pride,' he said. 'I shall never harm these people again.'

Krishna put back the mountain and the people returned to their homes. From then on, every year, both the mountain and Indra were venerated.

Why the Parijata Tree Came Down to Earth

During the churning of the ocean, the Parijata tree rose to the surface. The tree was unlike anything the gods or demons had ever seen. With exquisitely shaped leaves and curving boughs, the tree was beautiful to look at. As for its tiny star-shaped blossoms, they emitted a fragrance that perfumed the world. The Parijata tree mesmerized anyone who looked at it.

Indra had seen the tree emerge from the ocean and had claimed it for his own. He said, 'This will delight the nymphs and gods with its beauty and perfume the world of the mortals. So it should be nurtured in my garden in the skies so that all three realms might benefit from it.'

The other gods sighed. Sometimes, they thought, Indra behaved like a spoilt child—demanding favours all the time and sulking if he didn't have his way. Except that if Indra sulked, there would be no rains or he would go to the other extreme and send so much rain that there would be a flood.

So the tree was taken to Indra's garden. Indra's wife, Sachi, looked after the tree as though it were a baby. All the guests were taken by her to look at the tree and breathe in its fragrance that filled the heart with peace and joy.

Once when Krishna went to visit Indra, he took his wife Satyabhama along. Sachi and Indra received them affectionately. Sachi took them on a routine tour of the garden and showed them the Parijata tree. Krishna, who had seen the tree many times, took a deep breath of its fragrance and walked on.

But Satyabhama was seized by a great desire to have the tree for her own, and she was reluctant to move away from the tree. Sachi sensed that her guest was much too enchanted by the tree and tried to hasten her away. But Satyabhama refused to stir and Krishna had to forcibly lead her away. Back in the guest chambers, Satyabhama wouldn't eat or sleep. 'What is wrong with you?' Krishna pleaded with her.

'I can't do anything till I have the tree in my garden,' Satyabhama told him.

'Indra will never give it up. The only way we can take it is by stealing it,' Krishna said.

Satyabhama tossed her hair and snorted, 'So when did you begin having scruples about stealing things? Didn't you steal butter when you were a baby? Didn't you steal the gopikas' clothes when they were bathing?'

'But this is different,' Krishna said.

'I don't think this is different at all. Besides, you are more powerful than Indra and you should own the tree, not him,' Satyabhama added.

Krishna smiled. Even though he was no longer a young boy, mischief appealed to him. Besides, Indra was getting a swollen head and this would put him in his place. So Krishna uprooted the Parijata tree and took it away to Dwaraka, his kingdom.

When Indra discovered the theft, he was furious and led his army against Krishna. There was a fierce battle and Indra was defeated. As Indra, humiliated, turned to go back without the Parijata tree, Krishna said, 'The tree will be with me as long as I am alive. After that, you can choose to take it back if you want.'

The Parijata tree stayed in Dwaraka. And on the seventh day after Krishna's death, as the city began to be submerged by the ocean, Indra swooped down and took the Parijata tree back to his palace garden.

How the Kauravas Were Born

Gandhari was the daughter of Subala, the king of Gandhara. She was to be married to Dhritarashtra, the king of Hastinapura. She was a good woman, kind and generous.

At the wedding, Gandhari discovered that her husband had been born blind. Gandhari decided that she didn't want to see a world that had been denied to her husband. So she wore a blindfold over her eyes for the rest of her life.

One night Gandhari had a dream that she would give birth to a son who would almost entirely destroy the human race. She woke up shuddering and telling herself that it was only a dream. Soon she forgot about it.

A few weeks later, the sage Vyasa visited the palace and Gandhari, instead of letting the attendants take care of the sage's needs, did everything herself: from cooking his food to getting his bath ready to washing his clothes to pressing his feet to organizing the ingredients for his daily sacrifice. Vyasa was so pleased by her devotion that he asked her, 'What would you like?'

Gandhari bent her head and said, 'I did not expect anything in return.'

'I know that,' the sage said. 'Nevertheless you must have a desire.'

Then Gandhari remembered her dream and said, 'I would like to be the mother of a hundred sons!'

So Vyasa blessed her, 'You shall be the mother of a hundred sons.'

Soon Gandhari was pregnant. Unlike other women who had their babies in nine months, Gandhari continued to be pregnant for two years. Finally, she delivered a lump of flesh. 'What am I to do with this?' Gandhari asked herself in despair.

Just then the sage Vyasa appeared, and taking the shapeless mass of flesh, he divided it into a hundred and one pieces. One by one, he placed each piece in a jar.

In nine months, in one of the jars, a baby appeared. As soon as he was formed, jackals howled, donkeys brayed, the day became night and a wailing wind rattled the rooftops.

'This child will destroy the world,' everyone said, terrified. 'Leave him in the forest where the beasts will destroy him.'

But Dhritarashtra refused, and brought his son home. The child was named Duryodhana, or the one hard to conquer. A month later, ninety-nine other princes came forth. From the last jar was born Gandhari's only daughter, Dushala, for Vyasa believed every woman ought to have a daughter.

Thus were born Gandhari's hundred sons who were called the Kauravas.

How Agni Got His Strength Back

gni, the god of fire, was born from a lotus created by Brahma. His complexion was a brilliant red to match the vigour with which he leapt and flickered. Moreover, to keep up his strength he was provided with six extra tongues apart from the one in his mouth to lick up the butter offered to him in sacrifices.

Agni didn't demand too much from his devotees and so was a popular god. Lovers and men seeking to enhance their masculinity worshipped Agni and he never failed to grant them their desires.

Naturally more and more people offered prayers and sacrifices to Agni and soon he had consumed so many oblations that he became fat and lazy and lost his strength to blaze and burn. All it needed was a light drizzle to put his flames out. And each time he was invoked by his devotees, he found it more and more difficult to make an appearance.

What Agni didn't realize until much later was that the king of gods, Indra, had become jealous of Agni's popularity and had been looking for a way to humiliate him. Knowing that Agni had lost his strength to stand up to rain and wind and still burn tall and proud, Indra always sent a few rain clouds to put out the sacrificial fire.

'What shall I do now, Father?' Agni asked Brahma. 'I am unable to stand up to Indra. He turns up at each one of my sacrifices and ruins it. Unless I am allowed to complete a sacrifice I will not be able to regain my strength, and each time the sacrificial fire goes out, my devotees begin to lose faith in me.'

Brahma sighed, 'When I gave you seven tongues, it was to help you build up your strength. Instead you became greedy and ate up everything that was offered to you. You are paying for your greed.'

Agni fell at Brahma's feet and pleaded, 'I promise never to lose control again but please help me regain my energy.'

Brahma looked at Agni and decided that he was truly remorseful and meant every word. So he said, 'Go to Khandavaprastha. Krishna and Arjuna need your assistance. They will protect you from Indra. But even as you help them, remember that you could cause the other creatures there much harm. Do what you have to, but carefully, and when you finish, you will regain your powers!'

Once upon a time, Khandavaprastha had been a glorious city ruled by kings like Puruvas, Nahusa and Yayati. But the city had become a ruin now and in its place was a forest full of thorns and bushes. Birds and animals, thieves and bandits and murderers had all made it their home. So dense was the forest that those who dared to go in never found their way back.

Hoping to settle once and for all the quarrel between the Pandavas and Kauravas, Dhritarashtra divided Hastinapura. He gave the Pandavas the ruins and the forest of Khandavaprastha. It was here that the Pandavas had to build their empire.

Arjuna stood at the edge of the forest looking very worried. 'How do we build a kingdom here?' he asked Krishna.

Krishna smiled mischievously and said, 'Make an offering to Agni and he will be here to help you tame this wilderness.'

Arjuna set about preparing for a sacrifice to worship Agni. Krishna watched him and said, 'No butter or ghee is to be offered to Agni. He has eaten so much in the past few days that he has indigestion and will not appear anywhere food is offered. You need to light the fire with wood and scented herbs and it will burn by itself.'

So Arjuna did as Krishna told him to and Agni appeared. He rubbed his stomach that stuck out like a little round hill and said, 'Arjuna, I will help you tame this forest but you have to protect me from Indra's rain clouds as I go about my task. I do not have the power to blaze and burn as I used to. Even a little rain cloud can put me out!'

Arjuna, who was Indra's son, beseeched his father not to interrupt the mission and let Agni burn the forest down. Indra hid his irritation and agreed to stay away. So Agni unleashed his flames. At first, the fire burnt slowly and quietly but as his strength grew, the fire began to blaze furiously. Agni laughed in glee and leapt from branch to branch, from tree to tree, consuming the wood of the forest.

All the birds and animals fled the forest and the wicked men died in its flames. Just then, Agni heard a faint cry, 'O fire god, O Agni, we are helpless. Please do not harm us!'

He looked around wondering if it was one of Indra's ruses to trick him. Then he spotted a tree with a nest and in it were four baby birds. They were much too young to fly away to safety and had persuaded their mother to leave. Agni heard their cries and remembered what Brahma had said. So he left that tree untouched and burnt everything else.

When the mother bird returned, she saw her children were safe and she blessed Agni that he would never lose his strength again. Thus Agni regained his power and the Pandavas built their kingdom of Indraprastha on the ruins of Khandavaprastha.

What Draupadi Did to Feed Ten Thousand Sages

After another game of dice with the Kauravas, Yudhishtira lost his kingdom. He was forced to go into exile with his four brothers and Draupadi. During this time, he performed many penances. The sun god was so pleased by Yudhishtira's austerities that he appeared before him bearing in his hands a wonderful gift. 'Yudhishtira,' he said, 'this is the akshayapatra, the vessel of plenty. This will provide you all the food you and your family need for the next twelve years. It will fill up as soon as the food in it is consumed. However, once Draupadi eats her share of the food, the vessel will stay empty till the next day.'

During their time in exile in the forests, the Pandavas were visited by many people. Kings and sages, scholars and warriors all flocked to the Pandavas' simple home in the forests. No matter how many people came to see them, all the guests were looked after with great care and fed as much food as they wanted. This was possible because of the akshayapatra.

The Kauravas, especially Duryodhana, were very peeved to hear about how

the Pandavas managed to extend such hospitality in spite of having very little to call their own.

One day, the sage Durvasa came to visit Duryodhana, accompanied by his ten thousand disciples. Since the sage's short temper was well known, Duryodhana lavished much attention on the sage and his disciples.

Durvasa was immensely pleased and said, 'You have been very devoted. I haven't had such a wonderful welcome anywhere else. Ask me for any boon.'

Duryodhana sighed in relief. Then he suddenly had an idea. He would use this opportunity to add to the Pandavas' misery.

He cast down his eyes and spoke humbly, 'Your Holiness is very kind to offer me a boon when I was only doing my duty. My only wish is that you visit my cousins in the forest and honour them with your presence. Perhaps it would be best if you went late in the evening.'

Duryodhana knew from his spies that every day the Pandavas fed their guests first, then the brothers ate their share and only then did Draupadi eat. But all this was completed early in the evening, as the Pandavas rose and slept with the sun.

When Durvasa and his ten thousand disciples reached the Pandavas' home, it was late evening. Draupadi had already eaten, washed the akshayapatra and put it away.

The Pandavas received the sage warmly, not knowing that Draupadi had already eaten. The sage smiled at them and said, 'My disciples and I will bathe in the river. We are very hungry. Please ensure that the food is ready by the time we come back.'

When the Pandavas came to tell Draupadi of their new guests, she wrung her hands in despair. She did not know what to do. Durvasa's temper was renowned, and he could quite easily curse them for not giving him food.

Finally, not knowing what to do, she folded her hands and prayed, 'Krishna, only you can help me now.'

Krishna appeared before her. He said, 'I don't know why but I feel a great hunger. Bring me something to eat and then we shall solve your problem.'

Draupadi stared at Krishna in shock. What was wrong with him? Here she was asking him for help on how to feed the sage and his disciples, and he wanted food instead! Didn't he understand that there was nothing to eat? 'There is nothing to eat. The akshayapatra is empty. Which is why I asked you for help,' she cried.

'Go, Draupadi,' Krishna said with a smile. 'Go bring me that vessel.'

Draupadi gave him the akshayapatra. Krishna peered inside. 'Aha!' he said triumphantly. 'What do we have here? You said you cleaned the vessel but what is this?' He held up a grain of rice and a shred of vegetable.

Draupadi looked at her feet ashamed. He must think she was a slovenly creature incapable of even cleaning a vessel.

Krishna merely smiled again and put the grain of rice and vegetable into his mouth. When Draupadi looked up, he seemed satisfied with that.

'Bhimasena,' he called, 'go tell the sage and his disciples that the food is ready.'

Bhima stared in surprise at the empty vessel. He wondered what Krishna meant but went anyway.

Meanwhile, as the sage and his disciples finished bathing, they suddenly felt their hunger disappear. Not only were they not hungry, they felt really full and replete, as if they had just finished a large banquet.

'Master, we cannot eat anything more,' the disciples told Durvasa.

Durvasa too felt as if he couldn't eat even one mouthful.

Just then Bhima arrived to summon them to dinner.

Durvasa rubbed his stomach and told Bhima, 'It is strange but we are not hungry any more. Our apologies, but we will come another day.' And so they left.

Bhima smiled. By eating that one grain of rice, Krishna had satisfied their hunger, he realized. And so Duryodhana's plan to invoke the sage's wrath came to nothing.

The Killing of Kichaka

When the Pandavas were exiled for the second time, one of the conditions of the exile laid by the Kauravas was that the Pandavas should pass the thirteenth and final year incognito. If they were discovered before the year came to an end, they would be exiled again.

In the thirteenth year of the exile, the Pandavas disguised themselves and entered the service of the king of Virata. Yudhishtira was disguised as a brahmin gamester in the court, Bhima as a cook, Arjuna as a eunuch who taught singing and dancing, Nakula as a horse trainer and Sahadeva as a herdsman.

Draupadi, who pretended that she was in no way related to the five new servants, became an attendant and needlewoman in the service of the queen Sudeshna. She took on the name of Sairandhari and told the king, 'I promise to do my duties faithfully but I have two conditions before I come to work here. I will not wash anyone's feet or eat any leftovers.'

Her bearing and looks were so noble that the king agreed without hesitation. Draupadi realized soon after that this favour had made Queen Sudeshna a little peeved with her. Besides, she was so beautiful to look at that every man seemed to be attracted to her.

So Draupadi decided to allay the fears in the queen's mind. One day when she was combing the queen's hair, she said, 'Did I ever tell you about my husbands? They are gandharvas, the celestial singers. Though I live here under your protection, they guard me all the time. They are so possessive that they are jealous of any man who dares to look at me twice.'

The queen smiled, content that she need fear no threats from this new maid of hers.

For a while Draupadi and the Pandavas led a quiet life, each immersed in their new disguise. Then Queen Sudeshna's brother, Kichaka, a wicked and powerful man who was the chief commander of the army, saw Draupadi and was bewitched by her beauty. Soon he began to waylay her at every opportunity and began making improper advances. Draupadi didn't know what to do.

She first complained to the queen but Sudeshna ignored her. So Draupadi appealed to Yudhishtira. Instead of reassuring her, Yudhishtira scolded her for behaving like a child. 'You shouldn't take offence so easily. Besides, you can't keep running to us every time he mocks or insults you. Don't you realize that if we interfere, our disguise will be revealed?'

Draupadi went away quietly but she decided to appeal to Bhima who would, she knew, listen to her demand and fulfil it as well. So later that night she went into the royal kitchens where Bhima resided. Bhima was an extraordinary cook and so delicious was the food he cooked that the king wanted him to stay in the kitchen so that he was available to cook whenever the king felt like eating.

Draupadi walked into the kitchen, muffling her sobs. Bhima looked at her tear-stained face and asked, 'What is it, Draupadi? Why are you crying, darling?'

Draupadi wiped her face and said, 'It is the queen's brother, Kichaka . . .' Then she told Bhima about how troublesome Kichaka was.

Bhima bristled in anger. 'How dare he? Don't you worry. I'll get rid of him.'

Draupadi smiled. She knew that Bhima would help her. But she remembered Yudhishtira's words of caution and said, 'But you have to be careful. We don't want anyone discovering who we really are.'

Bhima nodded. He scratched his chin and said, 'This will have to be done secretly. Tomorrow you must set up a meeting with Kichaka in a quiet place. Ask him to come to the dance hall after midnight and then I will take it from there.'

The next day Draupadi as Sairandhari didn't move away when she saw Kichaka. Instead she smiled coyly and whispered, 'Come to the dance hall after midnight. I will be there waiting for you. Come alone or my gandharva husbands will know…'

Kichaka was so besotted by her that he didn't suspect a thing. That night, Kichaka went to the dance hall. He saw a veiled woman seated in the far end of the room and his heart beat faster. 'My lovely woman, why are you hiding from me?' he whispered. 'Come here, let me show you how I feel about you.'

But the woman didn't budge. So Kichaka shut the door and went towards her. He slowly took the veil off and there sat Bhima, grinning. 'Yes, show me what you feel about me and then I'll show you what I feel about you,' he growled.

Bhima beat up Kichaka so badly that his bones and flesh were mangled and then rolled him into a ball. Bhima was taking care that no one would attribute the murder to him. So he made it seem as though some creature that wasn't human had done this.

In the morning, the queen Sudeshna discovered her almost unrecognizable brother and began wailing. Her eyes fell on Draupadi and she shrieked, 'I know he's dead because of you. You must have told your gandharva husbands to murder him.'

Draupadi looked at her feet and didn't speak a word.

'Look at her,' the queen raved and ranted. 'There is guilt written all over her. She must be punished. Since her husbands killed Kichaka and they are not available to be punished, she will die with Kichaka. Burn her in the funeral pyre along with Kichaka.'

So Draupadi was dragged to the funeral pyre. The Pandava brothers watched in silence. Bhima and Arjuna looked at Yudhishtira's face, hoping he would say or do something. But he stood there quietly. Bhima could bear it no longer. He stormed away in a huff and rushed to the outskirts of the city where Draupadi had been taken away. He took on the form of a wild gandharva as he entered the cremation grounds. There he uprooted a tree, and using it as a club, he swung it this way and that scaring everyone away. 'Who dare hurt my beloved wife Sairandhari?' he roared.

'Sairandhari's husband is here. Let's flee before he turns us into balls of flesh and bone,' they cried and fled.

Then Bhima lifted Draupadi off the funeral pyre and wiped her tears away. Draupadi had thought that the Pandavas wouldn't come to her rescue. She and Bhima went back to the city separately.

Meanwhile the queen heard about how Sairandhari's husband had rescued her and she was much too scared to send her away. What if Draupadi complained to her wild gandharva husband again? So she left her alone, which suited Draupadi very well and the thirteenth year of exile passed with no further trouble.

How the Vindhya Mountain Became a Range

Agastya, a rishi, was born in a water jug as a fish of great lustre. Since at birth he was very small, even as a fully grown adult, he was a smallish man. However, his powers were superhuman.

Once in a battle between the gods and demons, the latter dived into the ocean and hid in its waters. The gods didn't know what to do so they went to Agastya, who they knew was angry at the ocean for some small slight.

'O great sage, please help us in this battle!' the gods pleaded and Agastya agreed. This way he would get his own revenge and help the gods at the same time.

So he stood on the shore, took a deep breath and drank up the entire water of the ocean. And the gods fell upon the demons and destroyed them. Meanwhile the ocean, penitent, fell at Agastya's feet and pleaded for forgiveness. Agastya relented and spewed the water back. However, since the water had been stored in Agastya's stomach, some of his juices mingled with the ocean water and it became salty forever.

Soon thereafter, Agastya heard about the trouble with the Vindhya mountain.

The mountain stood at the centre of the country, and was very proud of its height and bearing. It was so proud that it wouldn't let anyone go past it unless they paid suitable homage.

It was all right for the gods and the demons who possessed extraordinary powers and could find a way to fly above the mountain. But all others were at the mountain's mercy. Agastya heard from the other sages that Vindhya's arrogance grew by the day and he decided to teach the mountain a lesson. So he set forth on a journey to the southern part of the country.

When he came to the foot of the Vindhya mountain, he stood there and cleared his throat. From its great height, the mountain peered and saw that it was Agastya. Now the mountain knew that while Agastya might be a short man, his powers were immense and that, if he chose to, he could destroy the universe with his curse. So the mountain hastened to pay his respects to the sage. He prostrated himself before the sage and said, 'What can I do for you, O great sage?'

Agastya looked at the mountain that lay at his feet and said, 'I would like you to remain in this position till I return from my travels in the southern part of the country.'

The mountain agreed, thinking that the sage would be back soon. But Agastya had made up his mind to never return to the north. He settled down in a new ashram on Mount Kunjara and became the chief of all the sages in the south.

As for the Vindhya mountain, it still remains crouched. It has become a range of hills that are so low they can be easily climbed.

How Agastya Killed the Rakshasas

From his ashram on Mount Kunjara, the sage Agastya kept the demons under control. He let them roam freely wherever they wanted but as soon as they tried to conquer a region or its people, he would step in and destroy them.

The rakshasas Vatapi and Ilwala were brothers. They lived in the Dandaka forest. The wily brothers, who possessed many special powers, frequently tried many tricks on sages and other human beings, but Agastya always saw through them and punished them.

One night Ilwala and Vatapi were sitting under a tree. 'This is so terrible,' Ilwala grumbled. 'We are supposed to be rakshasas but we might as well be sheep. That Agastya has such a tight control over us that we can't do a thing.'

'What do you want to do?' Vatapi asked, amused by his brother's woebegone expression.

Ilwala smacked his lips, rubbed his hands and said, 'I'd like to kill a few hermits and I'd like to see every sage in the forest quake in fear when they hear our names.'

Vatapi thought for a while and said, 'I have an idea.'

The next day Ilwala disguised himself as a rich merchant and, leading a handsome ram, went to a hermitage. 'Noble sages,' he said, bending low and speaking in a very respectful tone, 'I would like to gift this ram to you. He is the finest ram in my herd and it would please me greatly if you were to accept him. He is worthy of a sacrifice . . . look at him. See how his horns curl so elegantly. Look at his eyes, they seem ready to face anything. There is neither fear nor stupidity there.'

The hermits examined the ram and decided to use the animal for their sacrifice. 'We are very thankful to you,' they said. 'You will be blessed for this generous gesture. What can we do for you?'

Ilwala looked at his feet and said, 'I do not need anything. Except that you let me stay here till the end of the sacrifice.'

The hermits agreed and went to prepare for the sacrifice. Soon the ram was led to the altar. After the sacrifice, it was usual to cook the ram and eat it as part of the ceremonial food.

Ilwala stood quietly, watching the hermits eat. When the last morsel was consumed, he clapped his hands. 'Brother Vatapi,' he called, 'please make your appearance.'

Vatapi, for it was he who had taken the form of the ram, tore through the stomachs of the hermits and came forth. As he emerged, all his different parts magically joined together again so that he was whole.

Ilwala and Vatapi looked at the dead hermits and rolled on the ground in glee.

'Vatapi, you are so clever!' Ilwala giggled.

'Oh, what did I do?' Vatapi said blinking his eyelids coyly. 'How can you blame me if the hermits had a spot of indigestion . . .'

Ilwala giggled some more, 'But I never knew indigestion could kill.'

Vatapi sighed and said, 'Now you know. What is it they say—you learn something new every day.'

Again and again, the two brothers tricked the hermits and killed them.

One day Vatapi said, 'This is getting to be boring. These hermits, despite being so learned, are quite foolish and are tricked easily. I think it's time we found someone who's a little smarter than these nincompoops. Let's try the trick on Agastya and rid the world of him.' Ilwala scratched his head and said, 'Are you sure? He is not like the others . . .'

'If you are such a coward then we won't,' Vatapi said.

'It's not that . . .' Ilwala began.

'Then don't make a fuss.'

So the next day Ilwala dressed as a nobleman and went to Agastya's hermitage leading a ram. As usual, he made a present of the ram to Agastya, who received it with a smile.

When the sacrifice was performed and Agastya had eaten the meat of the ram, Ilwala clapped his hands and said, 'Brother Vatapi, please come out.'

But there was no sign of Vatapi.

Ilwala clapped again and called in a louder voice. There was still no response.

Ilwala began to get nervous. He yelled out his brother's name. But Vatapi still didn't appear.

By now Ilwala was really scared and he called again in a trembling voice, 'Bbrrother Vvvattapi . . . ccome out.'

Agastya patted his round stomach and said, 'I don't think you realize how strong my gastric juices are. Even as I eat, my food is digested. Perhaps that is why I never have indigestion. Though I must confess that the taste of the meat I just ate makes me want to never eat ram again.'

Ilwala looked at him horrified. Agastya continued to rub his stomach and said, 'You think you are so clever but I knew what you were up to the moment you appeared at my doorstep. Your brother will never play his trick again. Do you hear me? Your brother has been digested!'

Ilwala lost his temper at that and raised his leg to kick the sage and trample him. But Agastya raised his eyes and opened them wide and stared at Ilwala. The fire from his eyes burnt Ilwala to a little heap of ash.

Thus the Dandaka forest was rid of the rakshasa brothers.

How Sivi's Generosity Was Tested

Sivi was the king of Usinara, a kingdom near Gandhara in the north-west part of the country. Sivi was a fine and noble king and his generosity knew no limits. In fact, his fame spread even to the heaven and the gods looked at each other in surprise. 'Could there really be someone who is so generous?' they asked.

'It is easy to be generous when you are the king of a rich kingdom,' Indra said.

'That isn't true,' Agni the fire god said. 'He is generous not because he is rich, but because he likes to help others. I have seen him give away millions of gold coins and they say there are no beggars or hungry people in his kingdom.'

'I'm sure he performs a great number of sacrifices which is why you have only nice things to say about him,' another god said.

'You know what?' Indra said. 'I think I am going to check the truth for myself. I will agree that he is truly generous when he gives more than mere material riches. Who will go with me?'

Agni offered to go along. The fire god was not too fond of Indra and wanted to see him eat his words.

'If we go as we are, he'll give us anything we want. So we need to go in a form in which he won't recognize us,' Indra said.

So Agni took the form of a pigeon and Indra became a falcon. The falcon began to pursue the pigeon and the pigeon flew into King Sivi's palace and into his bosom. King Sivi held the bird, which was trembling with fear, and stroked it gently. 'Do not worry, little pigeon, I shall take care of you,' he said.

Just then the falcon flew into the king's presence. 'Please let the pigeon go,' the falcon said. 'You are depriving me of my dinner and I have heard that no one ever goes to bed hungry in your kingdom.'

'Is that all?' the king laughed and said. 'I shall have my attendants serve you a fine dinner.'

'No, that's not all,' the falcon shook its head. 'I do not eat cooked food. I like my meat to be warm with life as I eat it. I like to taste the flavour of warm blood.'

'In that case, I shall bring you fresh meat,' the king said.

'That won't do either. I do not like others hunting my prey. I like to do it myself. So let the pigeon go,' the falcon said, bristling with anger.

'I'm sorry,' the king said. 'That is not possible. The pigeon has sought refuge with me and I cannot betray it and let it go.'

'Now I know that everything I heard about you is false. Your generosity is lopsided. You would deprive me of a meal to save another,' the falcon screeched in anger.

'That isn't true. I will give you whatever you desire except the pigeon's life,' King Sivi said, trying to placate the angry falcon.

'Would you give me some of your flesh? I do not need more than the pigeon's weight but I will be satisfied only if it's the flesh of your body,' the falcon said.

King Sivi nodded and called for a pair of weighing scales and a knife. Then he chose the meatiest portion of his body and cut a huge piece from his right thigh. The pigeon was placed on one scale and the lump of flesh on another. But the bird was heavier.

King Sivi cut another piece from his left thigh and placed it in the bowl of the scale but the same happened. King Sivi began to slice flesh from his arms, his chest, even his neck … Soon there was no flesh left to cut and the king placed himself on the scales. Finally the scales tipped and the falcon flew away.

Agni then took on his real form and healed the bleeding king. He blessed Sivi and went back to heaven.

'What do you have to say now?' Agni asked Indra.

Indra shook his head and said, 'I agree he is generous to the point of giving up his life, but what of the ones he loves?'

'Why can't you accept the truth when you see it?' Agni asked, irritated with Indra. And soon they began squabbling.

Vishnu heard their quarrel in his distant universe and sighed. If he didn't mediate and settle this quarrel, there would be chaos. So he called Agni and Indra to him and said, 'I will verify the truth for myself. But this will be the last time and afterwards the king is to be left alone. Do you understand?'

Indra agreed and Vishnu went to Sivi's kingdom disguised as a hermit.

Vishnu made his way to the king's palace. The king greeted him and asked, 'What can I do for you?'

The hermit cleared his throat and said, 'I haven't eaten for more than seven years and I would like to be fed.'

'What would you like to eat?' the king asked.

'I would like the flesh of a young boy, someone who has been killed and cooked by his own father. Could you provide me that?'

Sivi looked at the ground aghast. What kind of a request was this? What father would kill and cook his own son? Who would agree to that? Besides, how could he ask that of anyone? His subjects were like his children and it was his duty to protect them.

But he also had a duty to honour the hermit's desire. The king strengthened his mind, wiped his tears away and summoned his son. Then he killed the boy and cooked his flesh. He laid the table and invited the hermit to eat.

The hermit sat down and then said, 'What is this? I cannot eat alone. I would like you to share this food with me.'

'I am not hungry,' the king said quietly. He felt as if his heart was breaking.

'Even if you are not hungry, it is your duty as a host to listen to your guest,' the hermit said.

The king felt bile crawl up his throat but he swallowed it down and prepared to eat his son's flesh. With hands that shook, he raised a handful of food to his mouth. Suddenly the hermit raised his hand and said, 'Stop! Your test has come to an end. Let all the worlds know that there is no king as generous or devoted to duty as you are.'

Then Vishnu restored Sivi's son's life and vanished from sight. Indra and the other gods never felt the need to test Sivi after this.

How the World Was Drained of Water

Utathya was a brahmin who lived in a hermitage deep in a forest. When it was time for him to get married, he chose Bhadra, a very beautiful woman. Bhadra was happy to wed Utathya who was a good man, even though he lived very simply.

Varuna the water god had always nurtured a passion for Bhadra, but because of her father, Soma the moon god, he was much too scared to go anywhere near her. Now that she was away from her father's protection, Varuna decided to abduct her. So one morning when Bhadra went for a bath in the river, he swept her away and took her to his palace.

Meanwhile Utathya waited for his wife to return and when she didn't, he began to get worried. What has happened to her, he wondered.

He walked to the riverbank and there he found her clothes and jewellery. Now he knew for certain that Varuna had carried her off. 'I shall not tolerate this. I will bring her back,' he said. But to go to Varuna's palace demanding his wife back would be much too humiliating so he decided to send a messenger.

Utathya sent for the sage Narada, who was allowed entry into every world and home. 'O Narada,' Utathya said when Narada arrived at his hermitage. 'Varuna has abducted my wife and he has made her a prisoner in his palace. I would have gone myself to demand that she be released but what if he says no; then I will have to fight him and I am only a brahmin. I do not know the science of warfare. Please go there and ask him to let her go. I cannot be parted from her and neither will she be able to live without me.'

Narada was touched by Utathya's words and desire to prevent unnecessary bloodshed. So he went to Varuna's palace but Varuna refused to let Bhadra go.

When Utathya heard this, he felt anger build in him. How dare Varuna behave so badly? What makes him so arrogant? So Utathya, by the power of his penance, drank up the ocean. But Varuna was not perturbed and refused to let Bhadra go.

Then Utathya went to the lake of Varuna, which was the source of all water, and drank that up too. Then he cursed Varuna, 'Let this land become a desert and everything here will dry up and die. Only then will Varuna learn his lesson.'

One by one the rivers and tanks, seas and streams disappeared and the land became dry and fallow. Varuna knew he was defeated and went to beg forgiveness and restore Bhadra to her husband. Utathya was so pleased to see his wife that he forgave Varuna. He took back the curse and water and life was restored on earth.

Why the Cock Crows in the Morning

When Yama, the god of death and dharma, was a young boy, he was rather rude and arrogant. Though his mother tried very hard to make him behave better, Yama continued to be a nasty little boy.

One day, Yama's father, Surya, asked Chhaya, his handmaid, to fetch Yama from the palace. Chhaya went to the palace where Yama was playing with his pet buffalo. Chhaya said, 'Your father wants you.'

But Yama pretended not to hear her. So Chhaya spoke again. But Yama continued to pretend that he hadn't heard her. Chhaya lost her temper and she went towards Yama, shooing the buffalo away. 'Can't you hear me? I said, your father wants you.'

Yama stared at Chhaya angrily. 'How dare you shoo my pet away?' he shouted and kicked Chhaya.

Chhaya fell to the ground and was so hurt by Yama's insolence that she began to cry. The more she cried, the more upset she became and finally she cursed him, 'You

have to be punished. I curse that the leg you kicked me with be afflicted with sores and worms. That'll teach you to treat people better.'

As Yama watched in horror, his leg became a mass of sores and worms and maggots came crawling from it. The leg itched and hurt, and worse, it stank so nastily that Yama wanted to throw up. He burst into tears.

Meanwhile Surya, who was waiting for his son, came looking for him. He saw Yama's leg and understood what had happened. Then he saw Yama's tears and said, 'Will you behave better from this day?'

Yama, who had learnt his lesson well, nodded. So Surya said, 'As long as I am awake, your leg will be all right. But when I'm asleep, your leg will ooze and so here is a cock that will pick out the worms and maggots and relieve the pain and itch.'

Every night when Surya was asleep, the cock would appear at Yama's bedside and keep his leg clean. When it was tired, the cock would crow loudly and the sun would rise and Yama's leg would be healed for the day.

That is why the cock crows at dawn every morning, so that the sun god does not sleep late and cause Yama's leg to fester again.

Why the Moon Waxes and Wanes

Soma the moon god rose to the surface during the churning of the ocean and he was the guardian of sacrifices, penances and healing herbs. He married the twenty-seven daughters of the rishi Daksha and took them to his palace. At first, all was happy and well. But soon trouble began.

Soma discovered that he liked his fourth wife, Rohini, more than the others. So he spent all his time with her and gave her magical potions to make her even more beautiful. He took her everywhere he went and showered her with gifts.

The other wives grew jealous and one day they accosted Rohini, 'You are being selfish in keeping him with you all the time. He is our husband too,' they said.

Rohini sighed, 'I know, my dear sisters. But how can I send him away when he comes looking for me?'

Rohini did her best to send Soma away but in spite of that he continued to lavish all his attention on her. The other wives could bear their hurt no longer and went back to their father's home.

The rishi Daksha stared at his daughters in surprise. 'What has happened? Why have you all come back? It's only a few days since you were married. And where is Rohini?'

The girls put their heads in their laps and wailed, 'Father, we do not want to stay with him any more. He ignores us and spends time only with Rohini. It isn't her fault. She does try to send

him to us but he seems to like only her. So we decided to return home. Why live with a husband who doesn't care for us?'

Daksha was horrified to hear this and went to Soma's palace. There he advised the moon god to be impartial and love his wives equally, and treat them all in the same manner. Soma agreed and the other twenty-six wives returned to their husband's home.

But soon they discovered that nothing had changed. The moon still preferred to be with Rohini. So the wives went back to Daksha and this time he was so angry that he cursed Soma, 'Since you gave my twenty-six daughters only a fraction of your time, you will be stricken by consumption

and be reduced to a fraction of your size.'

Soma became very ill. All day he coughed and spat blood. He could neither eat nor sleep and lay on his bed wishing he were dead. Every day he grew thinner and thinner and his wives began to feel very sorry for him. So they went to their father and pleaded that he take back his curse.

Daksha shook his head and said, 'I can't take the curse back. But I can modify it. His condition will come and go, which means the illness will only be periodical.'

And so for a few days of the month, the moon is stricken with illness and reduces in size. Then it recovers and becomes whole again.

Damayanti's Swayamvara

Nala was the king of Nishadha. He was brave and handsome, virtuous and learned and very skilful with horses. Nala heard about Damayanti, the princess of Vidarbha, and fell in love with her merely by all that he heard about her. Damayanti too fell in love with Nala without seeing him. They wrote to each other, using a swan to carry their messages back and forth. And even though they never saw each other, their love for each other was complete.

Meanwhile the king of Vidarbha decided to hold a swayamvara. All the kings and princes were invited to the swayamvara where Damayanti would choose her husband by garlanding him. Nala too set forth to the swayamvara quite sure that Damayanti would choose him as her husband.

On the way, Nala met the four gods Indra, Yama, Varuna and Agni. Nala was delighted to meet the mighty gods and, as a mark of homage, he bowed before them and said, 'Your wish is my command.'

The gods smiled at each other and said, 'In that case, we would like you to go to Damayanti and ask her to choose from one amongst us four gods.'

Nala, having given his word, had no way of extricating himself from this mess. He pleaded, 'But how can I see her? She will be in her chambers.'

The gods smiled. 'That doesn't matter. We will teach you to be invisible. You can then enter her chambers and tell her our heart's desire. By the way, this mantra will work just once.'

Nala did as they asked him to. But Damayanti didn't know it was Nala who had come as the gods' messenger and sent him away saying her mind was made up. So he returned to the gods saying she was in love with someone else. 'But perhaps you should send another messenger whose persuasion skills are better,' he advised.

The gods smiled, having understood with their divine powers that it was Nala whom Damayanti loved. 'Never mind, we will take your form but you are not to let her know by word or gesture which one amongst us is really you.'

So the four gods and Nala entered the great hall where the swayamvara was being held and they were announced as Nala, the king of Nishadha. Everyone looked up in surprise when they saw five men, all exact replicas of each other. The audience held its breath. Who was the real Nala? And would Damayanti recognize him?

Soon Damayanti walked into the hall carrying a garland. She walked past all the kings and headed straight towards where the five Nalas stood. Damayanti's eyes widened. Then she smiled and said nothing. She looked at the five men and, without any hesitation, garlanded the real Nala. The gods assumed their real form and Yama, who was curious, asked, 'How did you know who the real Nala was?'

Damayanti smiled and said, 'My love for Nala is strong and true and I would know him even if there were a hundred lookalikes in the room. Besides, Nala is a man and I knew that the other four were gods. I saw how Nala's feet touched the ground and his body threw a shadow and his eyes blinked. I knew for sure that who my heart had guided me to was the man of my dreams.'

The four gods smiled and blessed the couple and left. And so Nala and Damayanti were united and they lived happily for many years.

How Destiny Overtook Parikshit

Parikshit was the son of Abhimanyu and Uttara. In the great battle at Kurukshetra, Abhimanyu, who was Arjuna's son, was killed. One by one, each one of the Pandava children were killed and the only child left to carry forth the line was this unborn child of Abhimanyu.

Aswathama, Dronacharya's son, decided to destroy Parikshit as well. He took a blade of grass, muttered an incantation and hurled it. The blade of grass fell like a thunderbolt and killed Parikshit, who was in his mother's womb. But Krishna came to the rescue and Parikshit was brought back to life. Thus the sole heir to the Pandavas was born. When Yudhishtira retired from the world, Parikshit succeeded him to the throne of Hastinapura.

Parikshit ruled well but soon he became so proud of his success as a king that he forgot the norms of good behaviour and became haughty and proud.

One day he went hunting with his friends and was in such high spirits that he disturbed the peace of the forest. He maimed animals, shot down birds, pulled down trees and soon he arrived at a clearing where a sage sat meditating.

He waited for the sage to greet him. But when the sage didn't, he lost his temper. He saw a dead snake lying nearby. He took the dead snake and draped it around the sage's neck. 'Well, sir, if you won't greet me with respect, this is how I will greet you,' he said with a laugh.

The sage opened his eyes and when he saw the dead snake he was

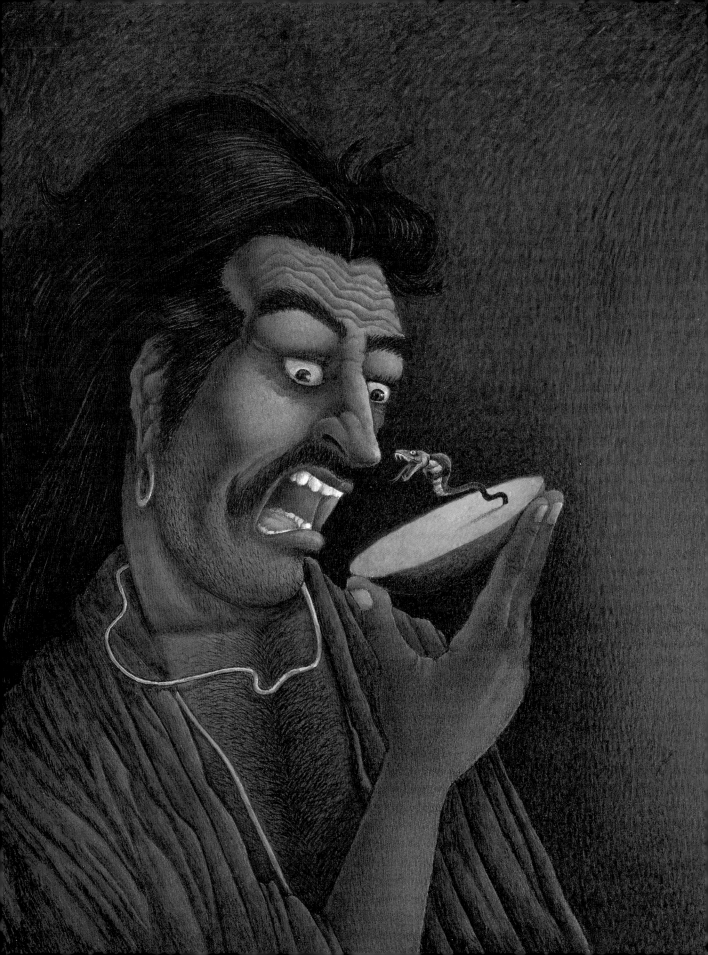

furious. He glared at Parikshit and said, 'Since you are so fond of snakes, I curse you that a snake will cause your death.'

Parikshit reeled in shock. He fell to his knees and pleaded, 'O sage, I must have taken leave of my senses to have behaved so badly. Please forgive me. Please take back the curse.'

The sage looked at the remorseful king and said, 'What is done is done. I cannot take back the curse. But if you survive for a year from now, you will never be harmed again by a snake.'

Parikshit thanked the sage and went back to his palace. He called the chief architect and had him build a palace of stone. The palace was built on stilts and it was impregnable. Neither serpent nor any living creature could enter it. 'I shall stay there till the period of the curse ends,' Parikshit said and he went to live in his stone palace.

Months passed by and with each day Parikshit began to feel less and less scared. Then there was just one day left. Parikshit thought, 'If I get past this day, I need never fear death again.'

Soon it became night and there were just a few hours left. Parikshit was unable to sleep even though it was almost midnight. Just a few hours more, he thought. He took a mango from his fruit bowl and cut it open. And from the mango emerged a tiny worm, which bit Parikshit, and thus the king died.

How Narmada Came Down to Earth

Shiva was meditating on top of the Kailasha mountain when suddenly Narmada appeared from his throat. She stood on his right foot and started meditating.

Many days passed and one day Shiva opened his eyes and was astonished to see a beautiful woman perched on his foot. Her radiance was such that she lit up the entire mountain range. She held a kamandal in her left hand and prayer beads in her right.

He looked at her and asked, 'Tell me, who are you?'

The woman bowed and said, 'I am your daughter.'

'What?' Shiva said. 'What do you mean by calling yourself my daughter?'

The young woman smiled and said, 'During the churning of the ocean you saved the world from disaster by drinking the poison that rose. And then you kept it in your throat. I was born from that poison.'

Shiva smiled and said, 'Do not call yourself the daughter of that venom. You are the result of the strength of my meditation.'

Then he blessed her, 'Henceforth, you shall carry the radiance you bear through the earth and bless the earth with your presence.'

And so the woman came to the earth as the river Narmada.

Why Yama Couldn't Ignore Nachiketa

Once there lived a great sage named Vajashrava. He had a son named Nachiketa.

Even as a child, Nachiketa was very interested in the daily practices in the hermitage. On his eighth birthday, he asked his father's permission to participate in the prayers. Vajashrava realized that it was time for his son to be initiated.

Vajashrava sent Nachiketa to a gurukula. He was taught the various sacred texts. When he was not studying, he and the two other students had to look after the cattle.

One day, Nachiketa saw some cows looking very tired. He wondered why. 'Oh, those cows are old,' one of the other students said.

Nachiketa said, 'How nice it would be if there was no such thing as old age!'

The other student laughed. He pointed to the sky and said, 'It's only in heaven that old age and sickness do not exist.'

Nachiketa was curious. 'How does one reach heaven?'

The other student shrugged, 'I don't know. No one knows, I think.'

On another occasion, a deer, who had become one of Nachiketa's favourite companions, would not get up from its reclining position in spite of his cajoling. 'Nachiketa, the deer will never play with you again,' a fellow student said.

'Why?' Nachiketa asked, perplexed.

'Don't you see? The deer is dead,' the other boy said.

'What is death?' Nachiketa asked.

One of the students there said, 'Death is when there is no life left.'

Thus started an argument between Nachiketa's two companions. One said that death is not the end and that life continues. The other said that death was the end.

This verbal duel stirred Nachiketa deeply. He asked his guru, 'Master, what is the truth?'

The guru replied, 'One must discover this truth for oneself.'

As Nachiketa was thinking about this, a message arrived from his father asking him to return home. Vajashrava was going to perform the Vishvajit yagna, the giving away of all of one's earthly possessions. This was considered one of the greatest sacrifices in one's lifetime.

On arriving home, Nachiketa saw how weak and thin the cattle that his father was giving away were. He feared that his father would be doomed to hell for such meagre gifts. Then he realized that this was all his father had and it made him sadder. Suddenly, he thought, 'I am healthy and strong. If I offer myself to my father so that he may offer me in turn, he may find the joy he's looking for.'

Vajashrava agreed to his son's offer. But now Nachiketa was impatient. Over and over he asked his father, 'Whom will you give me to?'

His father took this quietly for a while. Then finally, enraged at the pestering, he yelled, 'To Yama.' The instant the words flew out of his mouth, Vajashrava repented.

Nachiketa asked his father not to take back his oath. He said, 'Consider how it has been for those who have gone before and how it will be for those that now live. Like corn, a man ripens and falls to the ground. But corn springs up again in its season.'

Nachiketa journeyed to Yama's abode with his father's blessing. When he arrived, Yama was away and he had to wait for three days at his doorstep without food or water.

When Yama returned and saw the young boy and heard his story, he announced that he would give him three boons—one for each night that he had had to wait with no hospitality offered to him. 'Tell me what you desire,' he said.

For the first boon Nachiketa asked Yama to grant his father peace of mind and happiness. It was granted.

For the second boon Nachiketa asked Yama to teach him the sacrifice that would take him to heaven, where there was no hunger, thirst, old age or death. Yama taught the little boy all the rites and ceremonies associated with the sacrifice.

Nachiketa paused for a while before he asked for the third boon. 'Some say that there is life after death,' he said. 'And some say there is not. Can you tell me which is the truth? What is the secret of death?'

Yama was taken aback by the request. 'This is a question that even the gods do not know the answer to,' he said. 'Ask me for something else—gold, treasures, earthly pleasure, long life—anything your heart desires.' But Nachiketa would not be swayed.

Finally, Yama saw the depth of Nachiketa's passion for true wisdom and began to instruct him. 'Of the two paths open to men, the wise choose the good. The foolish choose the path of pleasure leading to a never-ending cycle of birth and death,' he said. He explained further and Nachiketa listened intently.

After Yama instructed Nachiketa, the boy returned home. The body of knowledge he had accumulated is today known as the Upanishads.

Anita Nair is the author of the best-selling novels *The Better Man*, *Ladies Coupé*, *Mistress* and a short-story collection, *Satyr of the Subway*. Her children's books include *The Puffin Book of World Myths and Legends*; *Adventures of Nonu, the Skating Squirrel* and *Living Next Door to Alise*. Her books have been translated into over twenty-six languages around the world.

Visit her at www.anitanair.net

Atanu Roy has illustrated over a hundred books for children and adults and has won many national and international awards for picture book design, illustrations and cartoons. *The Puffin Book of Magical Indian Myths* is his first major picture book assignment as well as the first time he has illustrated myths. Illustrating this book was like doing fifty separate books, he says. He has composed and rendered the artwork as paintings, incorporating classical styles of painting and architecture, and varied fauna and landscape as part of the art. He says, 'I have avoided the stereotype as far as possible and interpreted each story as only a story without any glorification or religious connotations. To the consternation of many it took me about five years to complete the book. Maybe I could have done better if I had more time!'

He can be reached at atanuroy1@rediffmail.com